GOD IS IN THE
PANCAKES

robin epstein

Dial Books
an imprint of Penguin Group (USA) Inc.

DIAL BOOKS

An imprint of Penguin Group (USA) Inc.

Published by The Penguin Group

Penguin Group (USA) Inc., 375 Hudson Street, New York, NY 10014, U.S.A.

Penguin Group (Canada), 90 Eglinton Avenue East, Suite 700, Toronto, Ontario, Canada M4P 2Y3 (a division of Pearson Penguin Canada Inc.) • Penguin Books Ltd, 80 Strand, London WC2R 0RL, England • Penguin Ireland, 25 St. Stephen's Green, Dublin 2, Ireland (a division of Penguin Books Ltd) • Penguin Group (Australia), 250 Camberwell Road, Camberwell, Victoria 3124, Australia (a division of Pearson Australia Group Pty Ltd) • Penguin Books India Pvt Ltd, 11 Community Centre, Panchsheel Park, New Delhi - 110 017, India • Penguin Group (NZ), 67 Apollo Drive, Rosedale, North Shore 0632, New Zealand (a division of Pearson New Zealand Ltd) • Penguin Books (South Africa) (Pty) Ltd, 24 Sturdee Avenue, Rosebank, Johannesburg 2196, South Africa • Penguin Books Ltd, Registered Offices: 80 Strand, London WC2R 0RL, England

Designed by Nancy R. Leo-Kelly

Text set in Century Schoolbook

Printed in the U.S.A.

1 3 5 7 9 10 8 6 4 2

Library of Congress Cataloging-in-Publication Data

Epstein, Robin, date.

God is in the pancakes / by Robin Epstein.

p. cm.

Summary: Fifteen-year-old Grace, having turned her back on religion when her father left, now finds herself praying for help with her home and love life, and especially with whether she should help a beloved elderly friend die with dignity.

ISBN 978-0-8037-3382-4 (hardcover)

[1. Assisted suicide—Fiction. 2. Old age—Fiction.

3. Amyotrophic lateral sclerosis—Fiction. 4. Dating (Social customs)—Fiction.

5. Sisters—Fiction. 6. Faith—Fiction. 7. Family life—Pennsylvania—Fiction.

8. Philadelphia (Pa.)—Fiction.] I. Title.

PZ7.E72518God 2010 [Fic]—dc22 2009033857

For my dad,
Dr. Paul E. Epstein, who is with me always

Chapter One

Here's what I've come to realize about perfect happiness: It's as fragile as the bubbles that form on the top of a pancake. I know a fair amount about the subject of pancakes because I used to eat them all the time—not just for breakfast. When my dad was in charge of meals, pancakes could and would be served for breakfast, lunch, snack, and "special pancake dinner" too. Whether we stayed at home and made them ourselves, went out for brunch at the local flapjack shack, or dined at that more famous "international" house of pancakes, I can say with confidence that I was quite the student of the pancake-making process.

But back to the bubbles.

When you make pancakes, you mix together all the ingredients and ladle the batter onto the hot griddle or in the frying pan. Then, the next thing you're supposed to do is to look for the bubbles to appear, because when the time is right, they'll float to the top and sides of the pancake. The reason these bubbles are important is because when you see them, that's how you know you're close; the time is near. It's also your cue to give those pancakes a flip, because if you don't they burn, and your cakes are toast. So those tiny bubbles signal everything's about to get turned on its head.

That's why the perfect pancake bubble can only exist for a small moment in time. After it serves its purpose, making your mouth water in anticipation of what's to come and letting you know it's time for its world to turn upside down, it pops and fades away. What comes next—how the thing actually turns out—depends on your variables: what you've added to the mix, how much you've stirred the pot, your ability to blend, its general shape, fat content, toppings, timing, and luck.

The comparison to high school is not lost on me either.

♪ ♪ ♪

"You have a bad attitude, Grace Manning," Mr. Sands says, his hazel eyes narrowing slightly as he gives me the once-over. "I like it."

"And you have a lot of hair for an old man," I reply, kicking the footrest of his wheelchair. "I think we should give you a Mohawk."

"A Mohawk?" Mr. Sands tilts his head back and curls the corners of his mouth into a smile. "Sounds painful."

"*Bok . . . bok-bok!*"

"Are you clucking at me? Did you just cluck at me, young lady?" he asks, trying to straighten up in his chair.

"I did."

"Implying I'm a chicken?"

"If the wing fits, Sand Man."

"Miss Manning," Mr. Sands says formally, in a tone I imagine he would have used in business meetings. "You are looking at a man who served in the First Marine Division in the Korean War, where I was stationed in the mountains by the Chosin Reservoir—the 'Frozen Chosin,' as it was known. The men of the First were officially called combat-ready soldiers, which meant we were the first on the ground fighting. Unofficially we were called 'bullet catchers,' because we gave the enemy something to shoot at. Over the course of my life I've been called a good-for-nothing jerk, a son of a bitch, and a whole lot of other things that would make both you and me blush if I repeated them. But in all my years no one but no one has ever called me a chicken. So go 'head, scalp me if you dare."

"You *really* want me to give you a Mohawk?" I ask. "Are you serious?"

"I'd say 'serious as a heart attack,' but they don't like people to joke about that around here."

Mr. Sands, a resident in the Hanover House Retirement Community, is one of the only people in this place who *would* make a joke like that, which is part of the reason he's my favorite resident. More accurately, he's my favorite resident *by a mile* and I'm not just saying that because he's also the guy who taught me how to cheat at Texas hold'em.

I've been working as a candy striper at Hanover House ("One of the premiere facilities for seniors in beautiful suburban Philadelphia!") since school started, the beginning of my sophomore year. That was when my mother informed me it was time to get a job because, "It'll help motivate you, Grace." Before this time I'd never realized Mom thought my level of motivation presented a problem. I never knew she'd given the subject any thought at all, for that matter. But even though I'd never admit it to her, I actually wanted to get a job. Having a built-in reason to escape the house a few days a week seemed like a pretty good deal to me.

Finding someplace to hire me turned out to be harder than I expected. I couldn't get work as a waitress because no restaurant wanted to hire someone who'd never waitressed before. And retail was another "no fly" zone for two reasons: 1. I don't care about clothes and 2. The girls who work in those stores freak me out. I always feel like they size you up according to your size.

That's why I applied for the job at Hanover House when I saw the ad on Craigslist. Being a candy striper seemed pretty low key, and amazingly, this place even paid a weekly stipend. Plus, I figured the old folks wouldn't care that my idea of dressing up is zipping my hoodie. The surprise was that I actually wound up liking the job. But that had a lot to do with Mr. Sands. I met him on the first official day of fall when I entered his room to water the plants. A troupe of local musicians who came to play in the residents' room walked in behind me. But they only got to the first chorus in "The Circle of Life" before Mr. Sands stopped them.

"I'm sorry, but my granddaughter," he said, tilting his head in my direction, "had a very traumatic experience at a performance of *The Lion King* when she was younger, didn't you, honeybunch?"

His eyes gleamed as they connected with mine and I took the cue. "It was terrible." I nodded, holding his gaze. "One of the giraffes lost his balance, fell forward, and took the whole chain of animals down with him."

"My poor girl learned the true meaning of survival of the fittest that day," Mr. Sands continued. "Now, I'm sure you don't want to bring up any unpleasant memories here, do you?" The musicians, who were usually greeted with big smiles from grateful residents, looked at one another, bewildered. "I didn't think so," he said, dismissing them. "Good-bye." Once the troupe was a safe distance out the door, Mr. Sands winked at me, then started laughing.

"Well, aren't you the good little liar," he said.

"Guess it runs in our genes, huh *Gramps*?" I replied, cocking an eyebrow at him.

"What's your name?"

"Grace."

"Frank Sands," he said. "How old are you, Grace?"

"Fifteen."

"That's a terrible age."

I nodded. "Tell me something I don't know."

"It's better than being eighty-four."

"You're eighty-four?"

"You were thinking I didn't look a day over eighty-three, right?" Mr. Sands grinned. "Hey, you play cards?"

"No."

"That's a character flaw, Grace. But don't worry, I'll teach you."

"I appreciate that," I said. And I meant it.

"You know, if this were a movie, this is when you'd roll me out of here and you and I would hit the road, conning people from coast to coast."

"If this were a movie," I replied, "I'd have better skin, a better wardrobe, and a cool getaway car . . . or at the very least, a driver's license."

"Details, honeybunch," he responded with a chuckle. "Details."

But that feeling, like we were characters in our own screwball comedy, remained. And from that day forward, whether we were playing cards or chatting, the conversation was always fast and fun between Mr. Sands and me. It just felt like I was a sharper version of myself around him.

I put my hands on my hips and look at Mr. Sands. "Okay, Colonel Sandsers," I say, "if you're seriously serious about this new hairdo, I've got some supplies in my bag. I'll just go get it from the volunteers' office."

"Colonel Sandsers, I like that," he replies. "And yes, march!"

"I will." I turn for the door, assuming we're both playing a game of chicken now.

"Good, and then hurry back, Gracie, I'm a decrepit old man and I have no time to waste." As I walk out of his room, I hear Mr. Sands yell, "Give me the Tomahawk Chop or give me death!"

I stroll down the constant care ward back toward the main reception area and return the wave of Patty Ray, the official greeter of Hanover House and keeper of all H.H. gossip. Patty has these Swedish-fish-shaped eyes and a friendly smile that encourages you to tell her everything, which she later makes public for anyone interested. She's always grilling me about what's new in my social life, and I always answer the same way: "Nothing, Patty." I'm a sophomore girl who's never been kissed (or even asked on a date), so it's more accurate to call what I have an "unsocial life." Still, Patty just waves her hand at me dismissively and tells me my time will come. Suuuure.

No one's around when I walk into the volunteers' office to get my book bag, which is good because I'd rather not have to explain "Mission Mohawk" to anyone. Hanover House isn't one of those high-security nursing homes where people watch your every move. They make an effort to let residents feel like they're still independent, even though a lot of them feel like they've been stuck here against their wills. "Like a prisoner at Gitmo," as Mr. Sands has said. "Like a sophomore in high school," I added. Still, you can tell that the brochure for this place, prominently featuring the stately front of the building, was created to ease the minds of the people who dump their aging parents here. Seems to me old people are basically like teenagers: Nobody really wants to see or deal with either of us, and when we're trotted out at family functions, the adults just have to pray that we don't say anything too embarrassing or offensive.

"Okay," I say as I reenter Mr. Sands's room, "I have some good news for you. And then I have some *really* good news for you."

"Good news first," replies Mr. Sands.

"Turns out I have absolutely nothing that will effectively cut or shave your hair in my book bag."

"Thank God," he laughs.

"*But*," I continue, raising my index finger, "here's the really good news: hair gel. Hair gel I've got." I unzip the front pocket of my bag and present the goop I keep in there for bang emergencies.

"Holy hell, honeybunch, you're going to make me smell like a rose garden, aren't you?"

"Yep, a very masculine rose garden. Now one final question before we begin."

"Shoot."

"Aren't you even the tiniest bit worried that if we do

this, people will think you've lost your marbles?" I fig-ure I should give Mr. Sands one last chance to think this through.

"Grace, they've been saying my marbles are gone for years, so what the hell do I care?"

I squeeze a big blob of gel in the center of my left hand. "But doesn't it bother you? People saying things like that?"

"Can't let it." He purses his lips. "You can't let what other people say about you affect the way you go about your business. You know why?"

I shake my head, then rub my hands together to spread the gel evenly between them. I don't exactly know how to make a Mohawk since I've only ever done one on myself in the shower, mid-shampoo. But it seems unlikely that Mr. Sands would have a "preferred" tech-nique for spiking his hair, so I just go for it.

"The reason," Mr. Sands continues, "is because peo-ple get things wrong. All the time. They get things wrong over and over and over again, and once you've gotten that figured out, their judgments or what they say about you seems a lot less important."

"So . . . what? You're just supposed to let it all go? Write everyone off as a moron?" I come to the front of Mr. Sands's wheelchair to see how the hairdo looks head-on. A little off center, and more like a faux-hawk than full-on Mohawk, but fairly respectable consider-ing what I had to work with.

"Not *everyone's* a moron," he adds, "and it's always a good idea to keep a few smart folks around to get a second opinion every now and again. That's what my wife and I always tried to teach our daughters. But for the most part, it's about following your instincts and doing what *you* think is right—your life, your control."

"*Ah-ha*," I say, "but then how do you know you're not one of the morons yourself?" I pull up the brakes on Mr. Sands's wheels and roll his chair over to the full-length mirror on the back of the door so he can check it out.

When Mr. Sands sees his reflection he starts to laugh. "Am I really supposed to answer that question looking like this?"

"You like?"

"The ladies in this joint are going to go wild when they see me!"

I can't help but laugh. "You're always working it, aren't you?"

"I've always tried," he replies with a smile. "Now my dear, I have a different sort of request to ask of you."

"Anything," I say. "Name it."

Mr. Sands pauses and waits until our eyes connect in the mirror. I smile at him and he smiles back. Then he says eight words that will change both of our lives forever:

"Grace, I need you to help me die."

Chapter Two

"Holy shit." That's the opening line of my prayer.

"Holy, holy, holy shit." That's line two.

I'm a little rusty at the prayer thing.

At home, kneeling at the foot of my bed, I stare up at the ceiling, but my eyes keep darting back to the corner of my bedroom where I flung my book bag. The bag that contains the pills Mr. Sands gave me to "help him die." I stashed the pills in the only envelope I had in my bag—the one containing the report card I keep forgetting to get Mom to sign. Since he no longer had the strength to do it himself, Mr. Sands asked that I chop the pills up, then put the contents into batter, so he could, in his words, "go out eating cake." He tried to make it sound light and easy, like a joke. But no joke could sugar-coat a request like that.

He said it would all seem natural, no one would ever suspect my involvement. Why would they? He said in anyone else's eyes he'd just be a dying old man who'd gone and died, and I'd just be a kid with an after-school job in a nursing home. But to us, it would be one friend helping another with a favor he couldn't accomplish on his own. So I left Hanover House this afternoon with twenty pills and a promise to Mr. Sands that I'd *consider* helping him with this "favor."

What was I thinking?

What the hell was I thinking?

Because if I know *anything* for sure, it's that I don't want to help Mr. Sands with this. I don't even want to *consider* helping him. But when Mr. Sands explained how the disease he has, ALS, was going to kill him—was going to take him out slowly, shutting down muscle after muscle, paralyzing each one until all that's left is a fully functioning brain locked in a body that can't move, communicate, eat, or breathe on its own—I couldn't exactly tell him that *I* was having trouble dealing with this.

He said he's worried about losing his dignity and becoming a useless burden. I couldn't even respond to that because all I could think was "But I don't want you to die." Then again, I definitely don't want him to suffer and *then die*. Which is why, for the first time since my dad left us ten months ago, I'm back here at the foot of my bed. Doing this. Which I'm not sure will do anything but turn my kneecaps into round red circles.

Dad was the one in charge of my sister's and my religious upbringing since Mom's never been down with the whole God business. She says she considers herself an "agnostic," which means instead of accepting that God does or doesn't exist, she just kind of throws her hands up and says, "Whatever." But my dad, he's a big God guy, so he'd take my older sister, Lolly, and me to church on Sunday mornings. After the service Dad would drive us directly to brunch at the International House of Pancakes. We'd sing a little, pray a little, then eat a lot and come home happy, full, and hopped up on Rooty Tooty Fresh 'N Fruity delights. It was our own little ritual.

When we'd get home Lolly and I would run around the house and Mom would inevitably complain about our sugar consumption. Then she'd say, "You are selling God through pancakes, Daniel." Dad, feeling pretty playful at this point himself, would always respond with something like, "Well, Sheryl, God created those pancakes, didn't He?"

But when Dad left us, I left the church. For me, the whole purpose of going got blurry. It seemed like people were preaching and parroting one set of morals in church and then practicing another in their own homes . . . and hotel rooms. It was hypocritical and it was phony, and it broke my faith in all of it.

And yet here I am.

On my knees.

"Look," I say softly, *"I know you haven't heard from me in a while. And you're probably mad. If you're even there at all, that is . . . But if you are . . . and if you're listening, I really need a favor right now: I need you to cure Mr. Sands. Please just make him well again. And then just send me a little sign to let me know that this is all going to be okay. . . . Okay?"*

"Grace!" yells a voice from downstairs.

Definitely not the sign I was hoping for . . .

"Grace!" the voice barks again.

Maybe if I just sit here very quietly, she'll assume I'm not here and—

"Grace, I need you to get down here now!" My mother was getting shrill.

"I'll be there in a minute," I yell back.

"Not in a minute. Right. Now!"

"Gah," I roar, looking up at the ceiling again before standing up. "I'm coming."

When I get down to the kitchen, Mom is standing there, tapping her foot, waving an orange ticket in the air. "Wanna tell me why I got a citation from the Department of Sanitation, Grace?"

My head is still spinning and she's yelling at me about something as stupid as a trash ticket? An involuntary snort comes from the back of my throat.

"I do not find this a laughing matter, Grace," Mom says, shaking her head. "Apparently the person whose job it is to recycle in this house has been throwing everything into the same bin outside, even though they're clearly marked and color coded to avoid confusion."

"Huh," I say.

"*Huh,* that's all you have to say?"

"Sorry?"

"So it's a question if you're sorry? Well, I think you

should pay the twenty-five-dollar fine. What do you have to say about that?"

"Fine, whatever." I shrug. At a different time I probably would have reminded her that sorting the stupid garbage isn't really my job in the first place. Recycling is one of Dad's jobs. *Was* one of Dad's jobs. He even used to say he liked sorting trash because it made him feel like he was doing his part for the environment. But when he left us—apparently not giving much thought to *our* environment—the job fell to me. More accurately the job was assigned to me, and I let it fall to the ground. In the ten months Dad's been gone, I haven't bothered sorting once. I just chuck everything into one bin because as far as I'm concerned, it's his mess to clean up. It's nothing short of a miracle that we didn't get that ticket before now. I consider telling this to Mom, but for some reason I don't think it'll help my cause. I reach for the cookie jar instead, and hold out a Chips Ahoy! to her as a peace offering. I know she isn't entirely responsible for this mess either. When she shakes her head, I give her the "suit yourself" shrug and bite into the cookie.

"Do you really need that?" she asks.

"Actually," I reply mid-chew as I hit the kitchen's swinging door open with palm of my right hand, "I do."

"I'll leave the ticket on the table for you, Grace," Mom calls after me.

Lolly's room is the first door on the right when you get upstairs, and when I walk past, I can see my sister lying on the floor with her feet up against the wall, cradling the phone between her head and neck. I stand in the doorway for a moment hoping to catch her attention. "What?" she mouths when she finally sees me.

"You going to be on for a while?"

Lolly shakes her head and holds up the "one sec" index finger. I nod. She's probably talking to Jake, the boyfriend. Lolly and Jake Davis have been dating for about three months now, which by our school standards makes it pretty serious. Lolly's annoyingly quick to drop Jake's stats whenever anyone mentions his name: senior, amber eyes, good hair, cute butt, good dresser, rich family. I know all of these things make Jake sound like he comes straight off the pages of the Perfect Boyfriend catalog, but what Lolly leaves out is that Jake's the guy who walks around with a perma-smirk and a sense that his farts smell like flowers. But I think dating Jake makes my sister feel important, so she stays focused on the pros.

"So, what's up?" Lolly asks after hanging up the phone. She pulls her legs off the wall and now lies flat on the ground, her long brown hair splayed around her as she looks up at me. From this upside-down perspective her chin looks like her forehead and her dark eyebrows make it look like she's working a partial goatee.

I walk around to the other side so the view's a little less freaky. "Jake?" I ask, instead of responding to her question.

"Yeah," she replies. "Can you believe he doesn't want to go to the spring formal?"

"But you do?"

"Of course," Lolly replies as if this couldn't possibly be a serious question. She sits up and stares at me. "You don't?"

The school dance that I won't have a date for hadn't exactly been high on the list of priorities. "I don't even know when it is."

"You do so. It's the second Friday in May. Why wouldn't you want to go? It's going to be really fun."

I know Lolly believes this. I also know she and I now have very different ideas of fun and I can't help wondering when, exactly, my slightly older sister and I morphed into such completely different human beings. Used to be that I was just a smaller version of her. We shared the same brown hair and fair skin, and because we were so close in age, it amused Mom to dress us in the same outfits to see if we passed for twins. Lame, I know, but whenever anyone asked if we were fraternal or identical, I remember smiling so hard, my cheeks ached.

No one would mistake us for twins now. Lolly wears tight-fitting clothes and makeup that makes her look like one of those pretty-but-trashy big-eyed Bratz dolls. I've been told I have the girl-next-door look, which I think is supposed to be a compliment, though I'm not sure why. Being "generic neighbor girl" never struck me as something to aspire to. That's why I started experimenting with the Clairol bottle the day after my fifteenth birthday. I needed some kind of change from the plain brown locks I'd rocked for the first fourteen years of my life. So I've been playing around with how much I can change it without my mother noticing ever since. I've been okay in the red direction, but when I streaked it "Butterscotch Swirl," I saw her squinting at me a little too close for comfort the following day.

"You can't go to a formal by yourself," I reply, "unless you want to look as cool as the kids who post their video diaries on YouTube."

"So ask someone."

"Who?"

"*Who?* Oh, come on, Grace! Eric." She throws her hands in the air as if this were the most obvious thing in the world.

Even the thought of Eric at a school dance makes me laugh. "Eric? Please!"

"You know you like him."

"Yeah," I say, "he's my best friend." Eric's been my best friend since we played T-ball together in fourth grade. Eric also happens to be a good-looking guy who doesn't know it and would never believe you if you told him—not that I've tested this theory.

"Okay, anything you say, Gracie. Anyway, what's going on with Mom?" she asks. "Why was she so pissed when she came home?"

"That's sort of why I came in here. I need to borrow twenty-five bucks."

"Why?"

"Because she's making me pay the trash ticket for not properly sorting our garbage."

"You're shitting me!" Lolly laughs.

"Could I even make that up?" I reply, shaking my head.

"She needs serious help," she says, standing up and walking over to her dresser. Lolly opens the top drawer and takes out her change purse, then pulls out a ten and a five. "This is all I have," she says. "But I need it back because I want to have money for the weekend."

"Sure, thanks," I reply. "I'm supposed to get my paycheck soon. I just want to leave the cash out for Mom tonight so the woman doesn't start charging me interest."

"Wouldn't put it past her." Lolly laughs again. "It's like she keeps getting crazier and crazier."

"I know," I say, "and it kind of worries me. What do you think it means for us?"

"It means we must help each other avoid becoming like our mother at all costs."

"Deal," I say, holding out my pinky to seal the pact.

"Deal," Lolly says, joining her pinky to mine.

JP JP JP

I spend the rest of the night in my room thinking about Mr. Sands and his request. But the more I turn it over in my head, the more certain I become that I can't do it; it's wrong.

It's just wrong.

I even manage to convince myself that he probably wants to take the question back. I'm sure he didn't really mean for me, a fifteen-year-old smartass, to take him seriously. Unless he thought that only someone with my "attitude" *would* do something like this? No. *No.* He probably only asked the question because he was feeling depressed today, and I understand that. Who doesn't have dark days? Who *doesn't* get crazy ideas every now and again?

You can't act on them, though. You can't, because what if you want to change your mind later? Plus, medical breakthroughs happen all the time. Who's to say that they won't find a cure for his disease tomorrow? And miracles. Miracles sometimes happen too.

Being optimistic doesn't come naturally to me, but I'm determined to remain positive. I come to my conclusion as I lie in bed: During my next shift at Hanover House on Thursday, I'll give Mr. Sands his pills back and tell him he has to fight this. Things can *and will* get better. They have to. I won't let myself think otherwise. I won't let myself think about his illness. I can't let him die. I can't let him go.

Chapter Three

Wednesday's a big day at Harriton High School. It's "VD day," as Eric calls it: Varsity Decision day. The list of guys who make the varsity basketball squad goes up this afternoon, and I know how hugely important it is to him. Still, after the tryouts on Monday, I wanted to play it off like it was no big deal, like it'd probably be better if he didn't make the team.

"Appreciate the vote of confidence." He grimaced, rubbing the bristles of his dirty blond crew cut back and forth and round and round. "You really don't think I'm going to make the team, do you?"

"That's not it. At. All," I replied, even thought it sort of was. Like I said, optimism doesn't come so easily to me. But I explained to Eric that *if* bad news comes and you're not expecting it, it's a double whammy. First, the bad news itself sucks, and then, when your legs are cut out from underneath you by surprise, it makes it that much harder to get back up again. So I suggested we meet up at Milk Bar, our favorite coffee shop, *just in case* he didn't have to report to practice. Eric didn't bother responding.

"That's cool," I said, "I'm not at all offended by how excited you seem to hang out with me."

"You know me, Grace. I'm all about the enthusiasm. In fact, if the whole basketball thing doesn't work out, maybe I'll try out for cheerleading!"

"If anybody can rock the pom-poms and hoochie skirt, it's you."

He clapped me on the shoulder. "I'll meet you at Milk Bar at four on Wednesday unless I need to report to practice. And if that's the case, trust me, I'll text."

♪ ♪ ♪

At 3:45 Wednesday afternoon, my phone's in-box is empty. When still nothing appears at 3:50, I hop on Big Blue, my aqua-colored mountain bike, and head for the coffee shop.

I love my bike. I don't even care that Eric thinks it's an embarrassment—he says I defiled it by swapping out its narrow, racing style seat for a fat, glittery banana seat. I tell him the new seat adds comfort and style. He says it made me look like a Mickey Mouse Club reject. It's one of those topics on which we've agreed to disagree . . .

I see Eric through the café's plate glass window as I lock Big Blue to a parking meter across the street. It's hard to gauge how upset he is because his head's down and his nose is in his magazine. He's never been a crier, so aside from yelling (which he does occasionally) and cursing (which, when provoked, he shows real talent for), I can't quite picture how he would react when he saw that his name wasn't on that list.

I want to do something to cheer him up, and since I can't think of anything better, I grab a handful of Haribo gummi bears from the package in my coat pocket. Then I creep toward him and at close range begin pelting bear after gummi bear.

"What the—" Eric laughs, his hands going up in a frenzied effort to swat back the bear bombs. "Oh, you are so dead," he says. Eric scoops up several bears from the table and fires them back at me. Every one that Eric lobs is a direct hit, mostly bouncing off my forehead.

"You throw pretty well for a girl," I say, both of us now laughing as I rub my face and sit down next to him.

"I'd say 'you do too,' but since that's totally sexist, I could never repeat something like that," he cracks. "Especially not in a hippie coffee shop like this, where, if the counter girls heard me, they'd probably start spitting in my chai."

"The counter *women*, Eric. The counter *women* would start spitting in your chai," I correct.

"Riiiight." Eric takes a sip of his drink from one of Milk Bar's oversized mugs and the bottom half of his face disappears in the cup. I want to bring up the subject of the basketball team and the list, but I'm guessing if he wants to talk about it, he'll say something. Plus, I'm not sure what to say except "Damn, that sucks."

I motion to the counter. "Want anything?" When all else fails, a chocolate chocolate-chip muffin tends to make me feel better, so I'm hoping the same will be true for Eric.

"Nah, I'm good, thanks," Eric replies, holding up his mug.

I return to the table a moment later balancing my wallet and the "bonbon du jour," a chocolate-dipped Rice Krispies treat in one hand, my cappuccino in the other.

"Oh, and Grace, in case you were wondering, only two sophomores made the varsity basketball team." Eric nods glumly as I return and am about to set the goodies down.

"Only two," I reply, giving him one of those *what can you do?* expressions.

"Yeah," he replies. "Just Mike Richter, who's six foot five . . . and me!"

"You?" I'm so surprised, my arm jolts and cappuccino froth spills onto my hand. "No way! So why are you here?"

"Why are any of us here?" replies my philosopher friend. Then, with a big smile Eric adds, "Practice doesn't start till tomorrow."

"Eric, that's awesome, congrats!" The moment calls for a hug, but Eric and I are not the hugging types. Instead I just give him an arm squeeze, and I feel a surprisingly firm muscle spontaneously flex under my fingers. "Why didn't you tell me sooner, you jerk?"

"Just wanted to maximize your suspense."

"Nice work." I shake my fist at him, but I'm the opposite of mad. This is huge and we both know it.

"Pleasure." He smiles. "And okay, here's something else that might be of interest you too."

"I won the lottery!"

"It's not that interesting."

"I won the school raffle?"

"Closer."

"Do not tell me that the creepy janitor has a crush on me," I say, narrowing my eyes at him.

Eric shakes his head, then leans in. "Four o'clock."

"Four o'clock?" I look at my watch. "What happened at four o'clock?"

"Not that four o'clock." He cocks his head back and to the side. "Just thought you'd be interested in seeing what's going on at four o'clock from where we're sitting. But don't turn arou—"

By the time he gives me the instruction not to look, my body has already boomeranged in such an incredibly unsubtle movement that my coffee cup skids and its contents again go sloshing over the lip, splashing the table.

"Smooth," Eric laughs as I stare at Natalie Talbot, the teen dream of Harriton High School, who is seated behind me to my left. Natalie's in my art class at school, but she's one of those people who seem to float above, possessing that combination of beauty and charm that bewitches both students and teachers alike. But right now Natalie's leaning forward and talking rapidly to her equally hot boyfriend, Rich Wilder. Rich is the center of the soccer team, and the kid who will almost certainly be voted "Most Likely to Do Anything He Wants." He's leaning back in his chair, his legs stretched out underneath the table, his right forearm resting across the brim of his off-center baseball cap. Natalie looks upset. Rich looks like he's asleep with his eyes open. It seems we're witnessing the breakup of the century.

"Wow," I say, "I didn't think people in *that* crowd were allowed to look so unhappy in public places. They're supposed to look beautiful, content, and above it all."

"Like beautiful people are contractually obligated to be perfect?" Eric takes the last piece of my RK treat.

"Precisely." I nod. "And from personal experience I can tell you it's a real grind. That's why when it came time to renew my own Beautiful Person Contract with America, I walked away. Decided showing my flaws to the world was the better choice."

"Good call."

"Hey, you were supposed to reply, 'Flaws? But you don't have any flaws, Grace!'"

"Dammit!" Eric says, smacking the table. "Guess that's why I'll never be perfect myself."

"That's okay, I like that you're a screwup. Gives you character."

"You know what else gives me character?" He smiles

and cocks an eyebrow at me. "Being one of the only sophomore guys on the varsity basketball team."

"That's true," I say. "Although part of me was hoping to see you shake your pom-poms on the cheerleading squad."

Eric picks up one of the gummi bears that had landed on the ground and then chucks it at me.

"I probably deserved that."

"Oh, you definitely deserved that," he laughs. I smile at him as I watch Natalie and Rich get up and leave the coffee shop, the two of them looking a lot less perfectly happy together than the two of us.

Chapter Four

In art class we learned a term called *trompe l'œil.* In French it literally means "to deceive the eye," and it's a technique artists use to create optical illusions. The artist does this by painting an object intensely realistically and making it appear three-dimensional instead of the flatter-looking two. What this does is to trick the viewer into seeing the thing as not just part of a painting, but as something real. For instance, a ceiling might be painted with clouds, a plaster wall could be made to look like it's constructed of stone, or a magazine cover might feature naked models whose bodies are painted to appear fully dressed. Part of what I think is so cool about trompe l'œil is that the way an artist achieves the technique is by mastering perspective, but the way a viewer sees it is by losing perspective.

It seems to me, we allow ourselves to lose perspective all the time, especially when it comes to things we expect or want to see. For instance, if you believe in something deeply enough, you'll often blind yourself to the reality of a situation so you can stay focused on what you hope will happen instead. In a sense, hope is the ultimate trompe l'œil because it blurs your perspective by mixing reality with desire.

♫ ♫ ♫

Though I'm not looking forward to the talk I have to have with Mr. Sands today, I'm not dreading it as much as I imagined I would. I think it's because even though I'm going to tell him I can't help him with his "request," staying positive and believing things will get better feels right.

When I get to his room, the door is closed. I knock and wait for a moment as I hear someone inside shuffling toward the door.

"Yes?" asks a nurse I don't recognize as she opens the door just wide enough to poke her head out.

"I'm here to see Mr. Sands?"

"Are you a relative?" new nurse questions.

"I'm Grace." No recognition. "One of the candy stripers?" New nurse doesn't seem impressed. "I was just stopping by to say hello."

"Uh-huh," she replies. "We're doing a little procedure in here now, Grace, so you can't come in at the moment."

"Oh, is everything okay?"

"We're trying to make Mr. Sands more comfortable, which he will be once we clear his lungs and get him fitted with the BiPAP machine," she says.

"Okay, I'll just come back later then."

New nurse looks at her watch. "He should get some rest, so why don't you come back another day? I'll be sure to let him know you were asking for him." She lets the door close between us.

I walk back down the hall of the constant care unit. I guess I hadn't realized Mr. Sands was particularly uncomfortable before. He'd been in the wheelchair since I'd met him, and over the past few months he'd get these random twitches in his arms and neck. But even though he'd joke about how he needed to get to the gym because his "pipes" were getting weaker, he never liked talking about his health with me. In fact, whenever I'd ask how he was feeling, he'd ignore the question. "Grace, folks here make me talk about how I'm feeling so much, I could star in my own TV movie on one of those women's channels," he replied. "So do me a favor and let's not talk about it." Then he'd switch the subject.

Between hands of poker we'd chat about TV shows (my favorite topic), articles in the newspaper (his), and occasionally the subject of my dad. I didn't like to talk about my dad and the way he left because the whole thing seemed so embarrassing to me. Dad just stole off one day and started a new life, as if Mom, Lolly, and I were mistakes he no longer wanted to deal with or look at. Actually, I wasn't sure who to be more embarrassed for—him, for his incredibly lame behavior, or us for inspiring it. But I wasn't self-conscious around Mr.

Sands and I started telling him everything, even about how for the first few days after Dad left I refused to believe he wasn't coming right back.

"Boy, I know that logic," Mr. Sands told me. "Refuse to accept the truth—simply ignore a problem—and you can make it go away, right?" He laughed. "Unfortunately, no matter how many times I tried it, that stupid trick never worked for me." He looked down at his legs, which no longer worked for him either. "But I get the impulse. And trust me, Gracie, you look around this place and you'll see a lot of similarly 'magical thinking.'"

Jeff Potts, the activities director at Hanover House, is in the volunteers' office, putting flyers in mailboxes, when I walk in. He's in his mid-forties but he still has the build of his days in the navy, and you can tell this because the shirts he wears are always one size too small. I guess he's considered a good-looking guy, and I might think so too, if it weren't for the finky mustache that clings to the top of his lip like a dying caterpillar. I can't help wonder why someone doesn't say something to him about that. But the old ladies love him, and I've often thought it's probably because that stupid 'stache makes him look like some 1940s film idol.

"Grace!" Jeff says. "How goes things? Good?"

"Yeah." I run the zipper up and down my hoodie, feeling more anxious than good. "I guess."

"You sure do sound convinced of that." Jeff laughs.

"Can I ask you a question?"

"You bet," he replies, widening his stance and folding his arms under his pecs.

"Why would someone need a bebop machine?"

"A BiPAP machine?" Jeff corrects with a smile. "Well, that's a device that helps with breathing, I believe. Do you know someone who's having respiratory problems?"

"I just went to see Mr. Sands and the nurse told me she was helping to fit him with one of them."

Jeff nods. Then, cocking his head to the side he says, "Grace, has Mr. Sands told you anything about his condition?"

"Kinda, yeah," I reply, not wanting to admit too much but wondering what Jeff knows. "I mean, he told me he had ALS."

"Right, ALS—Amyotrophic Lateral Sclerosis—is also known as Lou Gehrig's disease. Do you know anything about Lou Gehrig?"

I shake my head, and I think Jeff looks mildly disappointed.

"Gehrig was a famous baseball player in the 1930s," he continues. "Teammate of Babe Ruth's—you know who that is, right?" I nod, not willing to let my lack of Babe Ruth knowledge disappoint him further. "Well, when Gehrig contracted ALS, he was still playing ball, and he was at the height of his career. Because he was such a famous guy at the time, when he announced that he was suffering from the disease, he brought a lot of attention to it. Gehrig also handled himself with such dignity throughout his illness that he became its public face. So whenever people talk about ALS, they're linking it to Gehrig's memory."

"If I were Lou Gehrig," I say, "I think I would prefer to be remembered for my batting record."

Jeff smiles and evens the edges on the stack of flyers he's holding. "Batting records come and go. But when Gehrig marched out on that field in Yankee Stadium to announce his playing days were over, he said he still considered himself to be the luckiest man on earth. He talked about the opportunities he'd had in life, the strength of his family, and finished up by saying that though he'd caught a tough break, he still had a lot to live for."

"So he beat it!" Relief floods through my body. "I guess I was thinking it was supposed to be fatal or something."

"Well, no," Jeff says quickly. "I mean, you were right, this disease is always fatal. It acts progressively by destroying the motor neurons, which are the cells in the spine and the brain that control movement. Once those motor neurons are down, the brain can't communicate with the muscles anymore. So as the disease creeps through the body, those signals get weaker. And because the signals they receive keep getting weaker, the muscles can't respond as quickly or efficiently.

Eventually they stop working entirely because all the motor neurons—their lines of communication—are totally shot."

My brain shuffles through a group of images, trying to visualize his description. "So is it like trying to make a call with no bars on your phone?"

"Well, that's one way of thinking of it, yes." He smiles.

"But wait," I say, thinking it through for a minute. Though I barely pay attention in biology, I do remember my teacher, Mrs. Richardson, talking about how the brain controlled all movement—not just raising your arms when you want to raise your arms, but unconscious movements too. "How does someone with ALS swallow or breathe?"

"That's the problem." I watch Jeff swallow as he considers the question and his answer. "The person's ability to think remains intact because his brain continues to work perfectly well, but once ALS destroys those neurons, the person becomes 'locked in,' and can't do the other things on his own anymore. That's why we try to help them perform those functions with artificial means. Mr. Sands is getting the BiPAP machine because it will help pump air into his lungs as he sleeps. Apparently breathing on his own is becoming more difficult for him."

"Oh." *Shit.* Not the answer I was hoping for.

"It's a cruel disease and that's why Gehrig's courage

was so remarkable. We're all rooting for Mr. Sands to stay that strong too."

"Yeah." I nod. But what I'm really rooting for is divine intervention.

"We'll give him the best care possible. That's what we do here." Jeff runs his finger against his mustache. "You know that, Grace."

From what people say—and from what's printed on all its promotional literature—Hanover House is supposed to be one of the best old-age homes in the Philadelphia area. It has a leafy green "campus," and a stately, ivy-covered main building sits in the middle of it. It almost looks like one of the small colleges around here, like Haverford or Bryn Mawr. But I've always thought of the H.H. community as more of a sleep-away camp than college, especially for the healthy people who live in the cottages on the property. For them, Hanover House offers activities like art and dance classes, and occasionally they have field trips to the theater symphony, and the casinos in Atlantic City. Old people love them some casinos. Weird, but true.

What I find completely fascinating, though, is that just like in my high school, there's a social hierarchy here too. The healthy "cottage dwellers" are the cool kids, and they avoid the people in the hospital part like they're band geek losers. I rarely see the cottage people because I don't think they even want to tempt fate by walking near the hospital wing where I work; it's like they're scared they'll catch their cooties or something. The people here need full-time nursing assistance and are called the "constant care patients." When you're assigned a bed in this unit, you're no longer a person, you're a patient. You're "terminally uncool," as Mr. Sands says. He also says: "The only way people leave this joint is feet first."

As it turns out, that isn't exactly true . . . a lesson learned one afternoon when Mr. Sands convinced me to help him escape.

"Grace," he said, "I need you to help me bust out of this joint."

The path to freedom was fairly straightforward: I was to roll his wheelchair down the hallway, out the little-used and little-observed side entrance closest to the constant care wing, then push him as fast as my legs could carry us in the direction of the local cineplex, which was showing one of his favorite classic films, *Top Gun*.

Aside from a few minor bumps (uneven sidewalks and a disagreement about whether to get extra butter on the popcorn or not), the plan itself was flawless. Less flawless was our plan to break back in.

As I wheeled Mr. Sands back to his room a little over two and a half hours later, Victoria, a large nurse originally from Trinidad, was waiting inside, her arms crossed in front of her, her eyebrows raised in an expression that spelled trouble.

"Victoria," said Mr. Sands, honey dripping from his voice, "aren't you looking lovely today!"

"Don't give me none of that, Mr. Frank. Where 'ave you been? I've been outta my mind with worry!"

"Grace and I have been in the chapel. Praying," he answered. And I *was* praying. Praying he wouldn't look at me at that moment because I could feel the laughter rising in me.

"The chapel?" Victoria said, shaking her head. "Now you know I'm a religious woman. So I'm asking you, Mr. Frank, are you lyin' ta me?"

"Would I lie to you about something like that, Victoria?"

"Yes, ya would."

Mr. Sands chuckled. "Yes, you're right, I would! Well, you caught me. I broke the rules and I should suffer the consequences. I deserve to be thrown out of here. Honeybunch, just help me pack my bags and we'll go," he said, giving me a wink.

Not even the angry Victoria could prevent herself from smiling at this. Of course later I was given a fairly harsh talking to by the candy striper coordinator, and told that if I ever did something that was so "grossly negligent and dangerous" again, I'd be fired on the spot . . . Still worth it.

♫ ♫ ♫

I text Eric as I leave Hanover House later that afternoon and tell him to buzz me when he's finished practice, hoping we can meet up at Milk Bar. I could really use his company right now. I need the distraction and I know he'll make me feel calmer. Plus, time flies when we're together, and I'm more than ready for this day to be over.

My phone doesn't ring until 9:14 p.m., by which time I've finally settled in front of the TV to do homework. Lolly's sitting next to me and when I answer it, she shoots me an annoyed look that implies she'll never be able to concentrate on the TV show with me yammering in the background. I get off the couch and wander into the kitchen.

"Hey, how was practice?" I ask.

"Intense," Eric replies. "It was like boot camp. I think the coach wanted to see who'd drop first."

"How'd you do?"

"I dropped third," he says almost proudly. "Then Mike and I went out with a few of his friends for dinner."

"Oh yeah? Who with?" I open the fridge in search of something crunchy.

"Sam, Taylor, and the Roy twins."

The Roys, Chelsea and Cara, are identical twins who seem to be everywhere at once. They annoy me separately *and* as a unit. "Was it fun?" I ask, as if setting up a joke for him.

"Yeah, I had a good time," Eric replies. "And it turns out Chelsea Roy is really cool."

"She is?"

"Very cool, and pretty cute too."

This sounds suspiciously like enthusiasm. I shut the

refrigerator door empty-handed. "You mean cuter than her identical twin?"

"You know, they don't actually look that much alike once you get to know them." Irony is absent from his voice. "But man, I'm totally wiped, and totally screwed."

"Screwed? Why?"

"Since Mike and I are both sophomores, the coach paired us as practice partners. But the kid's the size of the Empire State Building," Eric says with a grunt. "I mean, do you have any idea how hard it is trying to keep up with him on the court? I have to run three steps for every one of his."

"Well, at least you *can* take those steps."

"Huh?"

"Nothing, never mind. Come on, you're going to be fine. You know everything's going to work out okay," I say. "You're a great player and you're going to be an awesome member of the team."

"You're full of it."

"You're welcome."

"Thanks," Eric laughs. And I smile, happy for the assist.

ℐℐ ℐℐ ℐℐ

I decide to dedicate the following afternoon to routine self-maintenance: The hair needs help, the face needs exfoliating, and the developing mono-brow needs landscaping. But midway through plucking my eyebrows into what I hope is the right shape—not too thin and U-ey like a surprised clown, not too straight and thick like a Hitler mustache—the phone rings. Mom.

She wants Lolly and me to meet her at 6:30 at You Say Potato . . . , one of the restaurants in the chain where she works as marketing manager. The office headquarters is based in the back of this particular restaurant, which more often than not means Mom comes home smelling like the day's special entrée. You get used to the garlic and Italian seasonings after a while, but the rubbed smoke smell is still a tough one to stomach. I tell her we'll be there. What I don't tell her is that Lolly isn't home, and though I don't know where she is, my money's on Jake's car. If possible, Mom's even less of a fan of Jake's than I am, so there's no need to serve up that can of worms pre-dinner. After hanging up with Mom I call Lolly, who answers on the last ring before voicemail.

"What's up?" Lolly asks. She doesn't sound terribly interested in my response.

"Mom wants us to meet her at the restaurant for dinner."

"I'm not really up for that."

"Cute, Lol." I lean into the mirror to check on the arch of my brow.

"I'm serious, Grace, I'm not going to go. It's Friday night. Jake and I are going out."

"Well"—I wince as I pluck a few remaining stray

hairs—"then you can call Mom and tell her you're not coming yourself."

"Oh, come on, it's no big deal, Grace. Just tell her when you get there."

"She's mad enough at me already."

"You owe me, little sister." Lolly's tone gets sing-songy, a reminder that it's time to pay up.

You Say Potato . . . is situated in a small strip mall on Lancaster Avenue, next to a dry cleaner's and a gourmet cheese shop. It takes about fifteen minutes to bike over, so I leave the house at 6:15 on the dot, not wanting to piss Mom off further. I walk through the restaurant toward the door marked "Private" at the back. This is the entrance to the room also known as "YSP Corporate HQ." There are three other desks in the room, but Mom's the only one still here, and her area is covered in paper, foam cups, and stacks of those oversized green and white computer printouts with the holes on the side, the ones that come from printers made in the dinosaur era.

"Hey, Mom."

"Hi, Grace, ready for dinner?" She looks like she's ready for a drink.

"Yeah, we eating here?" This is not quite as dumb a question as it sounds since Mom usually can't wait to get as far away from this place as possible.

"Unfortunately yes," Mom says with a nod, "because I still have a lot left to do tonight before I can come home."

"Ugh, sorry to hear that."

"Thanks," she replies. "But there is at least a little good news."

"What's that?"

Mom pulls her hair around to her nose and inhales. "Smells like today's special entrée is our favorite: fried chicken and mashed potatoes!"

It isn't until we take our seats in the booth that Mom eyes Lolly's empty seat next to me. "She with Jake?" When I nod, she shakes her head. "Be honest with me, Grace. Do *you* like him?" This time I shake my head and *she* nods. "I always get the feeling that he's trying to put something over on me, which is not exactly the most reassuring feeling for the mother of a teenage daughter. Thank goodness you're not dating too."

"Yeah," I say, making a face, "thank goodness."

The waitress walks over with menus and smiles when she sees Mom. "Hey, Sheryl," she says, "good to see you!"

"Trina, hi." Mom smiles back. "I didn't realize you'd come back from maternity yet."

"Well," she says, leaning in, "I hadn't planned to be back so soon, but Tim lost his job and I figured if I was going to be spending my whole day doing feedings anyway, I might as well do it in a place where I'd get paid for it."

Mom nods. "I hear you. Believe me, I know what the

juggling act you're doing is like. I remember all too well when I had to manage kids, job, home, *and* an unemployed husband who needed coddling yet didn't quite get that being out of work didn't mean he was on vacation from household responsibilities too." Mom blinks and looks back up at Trina. "But I'm sure Tim's not like that," she adds, as if apologizing for the comparison to my dad. "And I'll make sure they don't work you too hard here."

Trina exhales and shakes her head back and forth. "God bless ya, Sheryl."

"Leave God out of this," Mom replies, smiling. "This is between you and me."

Trina laughs. "Okay, well then, I'll just leave these for you ladies," she says, extending menus to us.

Mom waves her off. "Don't need them. You know what you want, Grace?"

"Yep."

Trina takes out her pen and pad. "Let me just tell you about today's special then." I eye Mom and we share a smile. "Let's see." Trina flips through her pad for the special of the day cheat-sheet. "Today we've got the chef's Southern specialty: fried chicken, buttermilk mashed potatoes, and creamed corn."

"Two of those." Mom nods with a smile. "Thanks."

♪ ♪ ♪

When I get home after dinner, I head for my room and my eyes go right to my book bag that *still* contains Mr.

Sands's envelope. I kneel again at the foot of my bed.

"Hi, I'm sure you didn't forget about my request," I say, my eyes flicking to the ceiling, *"but I thought I'd check back in because Mr. Sands doesn't seem to be getting better yet. And I just wanted to remind you that time is sort of 'of the essence' here . . ."*

The noise of a car pulling into the driveway below my window distracts me, and I wonder if Lolly will get in trouble later. I also wonder if I'd ditch out on dinner to eat with my boyfriend. Not that it's an issue . . .

I look back to the ceiling and refocus. *"Anyway, you know my mom doesn't really buy into this, but I really, really want to believe you're going to help Mr. Sands. I can't help him like he wants me to, but you, you could fix it so he wouldn't even have to think about that . . . And then I wouldn't have to think about it either . . . So just please make him well again, okay? Please."* I close my eyes as if trying to seal up the wish and send it out to the universe.

Chapter Five

When I get to the volunteers' office on Tuesday I see I've been assigned to magazine duty on the new weekly schedule, so I load the mags in my book bag and start walking the corridors. Celebrity magazines get a bad rap in my opinion. I understand that they're not particularly intellectual or enlightening, but sometimes I think they're better than that. Sometimes they provide even what a "great book" can't: instantaneous escape. True, I've always had a weakness for celebrity gossip, but I only realized how important it could be when I started working at Hanover House. One of the candy striper's jobs is "magazine detail," and armed with stories of teen idols, baby bumps, reality show scandals, starlet diets, and divorces, we hand out the latest editions to residents and their families. Sometimes people turn their noses up when I offer them, but mostly folks seem to be happy to be provided with something new to talk about and something mindless to focus on—particularly when it's someone else's problems. So if these magazines help them laugh at someone rich and famous, someone who seems to have it all when they themselves are losing it, I think that's worth far more than the subscription price.

I purposefully leave Mr. Sands's room for last since I still haven't gotten the chance to tell him what I'd decided and to make him agree to hang on and fight. And this way, once I finish handing out the magazines, I can spend the rest of my shift with him.

I run through the rounds as quickly as I can, practically throwing copies of *Us Weekly, Life and Style,* and *Star* at people paperboy style. When I finally exhaust my supply, I head for Mr. Sands's room. "Hey!" I say, striding into the Sands Castle. But when I see him, I stop short: Mr. Sands is lying in bed with tubes sticking in and out of his arms and around his nose and neck.

"Grace, look at what they've done to me," he says softly, his voice sounding nasal. Then he laughs a bit and I can tell he's trying to keep things light.

"Who's responsible for this?" I point to the clear-colored tubing encircling him. "Because it looks like the work of Spider-Man!"

"Just the nurses," he says. "I think they were trying to teach me a lesson."

Smiling, I lean in conspiratorially. "You've really got to stop harassing them."

"Party pooper."

I pull up a chair to his bed and sit down. "I tried to stop by last week because I wanted to talk to you, but you were having a procedure done. You feeling okay?"

"Well, I'm better now that you're here, honeybunch."

He smiles, his voice still quiet. "And I have a feeling I know what you want to talk about. Why don't you close the door?"

I nod, suddenly nervous, latch the door closed, and lean against the wall next to Mr. Sands's bed. "Yeah," I say, unsure of how to start but knowing this is something I don't want to joke about. "So that thing you asked me to help you with last week?"

"Yes," he replies.

"Um, yeah. I just—" My mouth is dry, but when I swallow, it doesn't help. I just feel my throat moving up and down. Actually having to do this face-to-face is much harder than just rehearsing it to myself, and for the first time with Mr. Sands, the words aren't coming naturally to me. Nothing feels natural about this at all. I try again: "So the thing is, I don't really think what you asked me to do is a good idea." I pause, waiting for him to jump in. He doesn't. "I mean, you've got to keep fighting because you just never know when they may find a cure for you."

His expression changes only slightly, like he'd been steeling himself for this response. "It was a mistake," he replies.

I exhale. "Okay, so you don't think it's a good idea anymore either, do you? I mean, you don't want to—" I struggle even to say the word.

"No, I haven't changed my mind about that, honey. Death doesn't scare me. It's the living hell that comes before it that does . . ." Mr. Sands trails off. "But fear got the better of me when I asked you to help me. It was weak. Terribly weak of me," he says. "I shouldn't have burdened you with this—I can't tell you how sorry I am that I did. All of this is just making me crazy. I'm losing it, Gracie. I'm losing . . . everything."

"But anything can happen." I'm nodding rapidly, as if trying to erase the look of desperation painted on Mr. Sands's face. "Things can change."

"I'm glad you think that, I really am." There's resignation in his tone. "But, if you have those pills on you, you can just tuck the envelope in the top drawer of my night-stand. And then let's just try to forget this, okay?"

I don't know what else to say, so I unzip the front pocket of my book bag and remove the envelope. Then I open the drawer and slide the envelope to the very back, under a few old magazines and assorted clippings.

"That's fine," he says after I close the drawer and turn back to him. "Now tell me some good news, honey-bunch, I could use it."

"Good news . . . good news . . ." I have to think about this for a moment since nothing particularly cheery springs to mind, and I'm still feeling the sting that I've failed Mr. Sands. "Oh, okay, well, this is sort of funny. My mom got really pissed at me the other night because I didn't sort the recyclables and she got a ticket from the Sanitation Department. She was so mad, I thought her head was going to explode."

"Grace," Mr. Sands says, and from the fatherly tone of his voice, it's clear he doesn't approve. But he doesn't scold, he just leaves it at that.

♩ ♩ ♩

When I leave Hanover House that afternoon, I head directly for the Fulton Pharmacy. As soon as I buy the package of M&M'S I've been craving, I start loading them into my mouth like I'm filling a Pez dispenser. I can't stop thinking about the food they brought to him as I was leaving. Mr. Sands's meal—if you can call it that—was an assortment of variously colored mush, shaped to resemble a slice of meatloaf, a helping of peas, mashed potatoes, and applesauce. As we watched the nurse set the tray in front of him he shot me a "get me the hell out of here!" glance. Who could blame him?

I do my best to focus only on the M&M'S. I don't want to think about the destruction of Mr. Sands's motor neurons. I don't want to think about full body paralysis. And I don't want to think about the brave dead baseball player who set the "right" example for dealing with the disease.

♩ ♩ ♩

It's past dusk as I ride down Shrader Lane. The street, chockablock with row homes—none of which looks particularly inviting in the daytime—seems even more intimidating in the fading light. I ring the doorbell of

Eric's house and open the screen door expecting him to come bounding down the stairs—as if he'd somehow sense my arrival. But instead it's Eric's mother who answers.

"Well hello, hello!" she says warmly. "Come on in, Grace, I didn't know Eric was expecting you."

"Actually, he isn't," I reply. "I'm just kind of dropping by."

"Eric's been playing video games upstairs for the past several hours, so some human contact will do him good. He nearly killed me when I interrupted to tell him Chelsea Roy was on the phone waiting for him to pick up."

"That's funny," I say, more surprised by Chelsea's call than Eric's reaction.

Mrs. Ward smiles and it's not hard to see where Eric gets his looks from. She doesn't wear much makeup or anything, but I have a feeling if she got all glammed out she could be movie star pretty. Plus she has this amazing chestnutty-red hair, which might be natural or could just as easily come from a box, but whichever it is, I'm going to try to duplicate it the next time I experiment.

"Go on up," she says. "Oh, and Grace, have you had dinner? Do you want to bring a snack up there for yourself?"

"I'm good, thanks, Mrs. Ward," I reply, holding out my bag of M&M'S to her. "You want some?"

"I shouldn't," she says with a frown, "I'm trying to be good."

"Being good's overrated," I say, and she laughs.

I knock on Eric's door and when he doesn't answer, I walk in anyway. Just as expected, he's staring at his screen, headphones on, mouth slightly open, deep in the puzzle-plagued land of Zelda.

"Hey." I tap him on the shoulder.

Eric jumps slightly at my touch. "Oh, hey," he says, keeping his eyes fixed on the screen. "What's up?"

"You ever heard of Lou Gehrig?" I say, flopping down on his bed and staring up at the ceiling.

"Yeah, sure. Why?" Eric asks, briefly turning around to look at me.

"You know about that disease he had?"

"Lou Gehrig's disease?"

"Good guess. So what do you know about it?"

"Well, I've *heard* of it, but that's about it," he says, turning back to the screen to make sure neither he nor his princess meets with his own untimely fate.

I lie back on his bed and stare at the light fixture in the center of his ceiling. A gross number of dead bugs have collected in the glass bubble. "You know you should really clean that light out," I say. "It's bug hell up there."

"I prefer to think of it as atmosphere," he replies.

"So did you read the next chapter in *As You Like It* yet?"

"Nope."

"Oh." I wait to get Eric's attention, but when I look

at the screen, I can see he's at a level he doesn't usually get to, and that his house would pretty much have to be burning down to get him to stop playing at this point. I might get a reaction if I asked about *Chelsea*, but instead I get off the bed and stand behind him. I hover over his chair and put my hands on its arms. As I take a breath, I inhale the scent of his soap. I close my eyes and lean closer. The smell is familiar, but what I'm feeling is not. The closeness makes my skin tingle.

"Hey, come on," he laughs sensing my proximity, and bats his hand behind him. "You trying to throw off my game?"

I don't move. I don't want to move. What occurs to me at that moment is that what I really want to do is just lean against Eric. I want him to put his arms around me. I want him to tell me everything's going to be okay. And I don't want him to let go.

"Grace, seriously," he says, his shoulders tensing. Though he's not facing me, I know Eric's not looking at the screen anymore either, because when I look forward, the hero, Link, is just standing in the woods, no longer moving, also appearing uncertain of his next move.

"Sorry." I quickly back away, trying to recover. "I guess I'm still a little shaky from being at Hanover House." I sit down on the edge of the bed and prop my elbows on my knees.

Eric finally puts the game on pause and turns to look at me. "Why? What happened?"

"Well, that resident I always talk about, Mr. Sands—"

"The guy who taught you how to play cards?"

"Yeah. So he's the one with Lou Gehrig's disease, and I think he's really starting to go downhill."

"How much time does he have left?"

"Don't know." I shake my head. "The only thing they do know is that he's just going to get worse and worse, and they can't do anything to stop it."

"That sucks. I'm sorry, Grace."

I consider telling Eric what Mr. Sands asked me to do, and I wonder how he would respond. But I decide not to say anything—to him or anyone else—because I think it would be like telling someone's most personal secret, which is the last thing I'd want to do. It would also expose him to other people's judgments, and it doesn't matter what anyone else thinks. This is about what Mr. Sands wants.

"Yeah," I say, my stomach knotted with a variety of feelings, "I'm sorry too."

Chapter Six

Surprises are a funny thing. When I was younger, I loved them. I couldn't imagine anything better, and I couldn't get enough of them. That's probably because back then, surprises mostly came wrapped in brightly colored boxes, tied with silky ribbons. A surprise could also be a fuzzy little animal pulled from a magician's top hat. Or a sweet-tasting candy-coated reward that turned my tongue and teeth exotic shades of the rainbow. But whatever it was, the surprise almost always came with a smile that seemed like a promise: This thing that you hadn't even seen was going to make your day better.

The surprises I've had recently have been an entirely different variety. They're the pop quizzes I'm not prepared for. Fights I didn't see brewing. Appearances and disappearances of people whose smiles mean squat. These surprises make me feel like *I'm* that poor fuzzy bunny who's being yanked around by the ears.

When my cell phone rings ten minutes after school ends, I look at the call screen and get another surprise. "DAD," it reads, like a punch to the gut.

I drop the phone back into my book bag and continue unlocking Big Blue from the school bike rack. I hop on my bike and don't stop pedaling even when the alert of a new voicemail sounds. It only makes me pedal faster toward Hanover House, despite the fact that I now feel the contents of my lunch rumbling around in my stomach.

Dad has left messages before. But I've always deleted them. When I pull into the Hanover House parking lot, I hop off my bike, thread the lock through the front wheel, and leave it in the space next to Jeff Potts's cherry red Kawasaki motorcycle. It's only when I get to the big porch on the main building that I take the cell out of my bag and look at the flashing red message icon.

I exhale, then hit the voicemail button, deciding today is the day I'll finally listen to what he has to say for himself.

"Hi, Grace, it's me . . . Dad? Remember m—"

Delete.

The ladies' room isn't far, but I wonder if I'll be able to make it there without throwing up. Thankfully I manage to get into a stall, turn around, and bend over the toilet before the contents of my stomach come heaving out of my throat. I spit the metallic remains of stomach acid and nasty school lunch into the bowl before flushing the toilet. When I'm sure my stomach is entirely empty, I flip down the lid of the toilet and stand on the seat. Crouching on top of the bowl, I grip my hands around my stomach and rock back and forth trying to recover from this shock to my system.

"Come on!" I say, looking up, angry now. *"What is going on here? Are you doing this for some special reason?"*

"Wouldn't be any fun if you knew the plan," a voice replies.

I'm so rattled by the sound of the voice I lose my footing on the toilet seat and bang my hip against the metal toilet paper roll. When I get back on my feet, I open the door and see an old woman with bright white hair pinned in a loose bun at the top of her head. Her hand is up to her mouth and from the crinkle around her eyes, it's pretty clear she finds this all very amusing.

"Forgive me," the woman says. "I think I interrupted you in a private moment."

"Well," I reply, instead of yelling something to the effect of: "No kidding, lady, I'm in the bathroom!"

"Were you praying?" she asks.

"Sort of."

"That's what I thought," the woman says with a nod, "which is why I spoke up. I like the idea of answering prayers," she says. "Plus, I figure I'm so old, I could have been God's babysitter."

I look at her and she's smiling. I can't help but laugh a little myself.

"Good," the old woman replies, "I'm glad you laughed. You know, a lot of people around here don't have any sense of humor at all. They would have said, 'Oh, you're not that old!' And then I'd have to explain that I know I'm not *that* old, I was merely trying to make a joke, which would make the whole thing just absurd. When you have to explain why something's funny . . ." She trails off. "You know what I mean?"

"Too well," I reply, smiling. I can't remember any of the other lady residents making me laugh—especially not in a place or time like this. I stare at the woman and try to place her, but she doesn't look familiar to me. "Did you just move to Hanover House?" I ask.

"No, I'm part of the cottage community around back."

"Oh, are you sick?" She doesn't look sick, but I think sometimes it can be hard to tell with old people, and I wonder how this would affect her status as one of the cottage folk cool kids.

"No," she replies, pausing and looking down in a way that makes me realize I probably shouldn't have asked the question. "Just visiting. But how rude of me! I don't think I introduced myself. I'm Isabelle." She straightens her back a bit, then extends her hand to me.

"I'm Grace," I reply, returning her surprisingly firm handshake. It sort of feels like the woman could crush rocks if she—

"Grace!" Isabelle says. A mischievous smile reappears and makes me wonder if she's about to make a pun on my name. Everyone thinks they're the first to tell me *"You don't look graceful."* Instead she simply says, "Well, it's so nice to meet you officially. I've heard great things about you."

"You have?"

Isabelle nods. "You shouldn't sound that surprised," she says, "it's a dead giveaway that you're really an awful person."

"What?"

"Grace, I'm teasing you!" Isabelle laughs. "What happened to that sense of humor you had a minute ago?"

"Sorry, I guess I'm a little off today."

"Mmm, I've had a lot of those days recently," she responds. "Anyway, my husband mentioned you by name to me, which means he thinks you're quite special—my husband never remembers anyone's name."

"Oh, thank you." I smile.

"I'm heading home now," Isabelle says. "But if you have a moment, please come visit us."

"Sure," I reply. "What's the room number again?" I think this is a pretty clever way of getting out of admitting that though I may have made some sort of impression on her husband, he was just a muddle of white hair and wrinkles to me.

"Three twenty-three. Wait." She pauses. "Is that right? Maybe it's two thirty-two. Numbers confuse the hell out of me, always have, and don't let them convince you that trigonometry will ever be important in your life. It's a damn lie."

"I always had that suspicion." I nod, deciding that

whatever else I was supposed to be doing, I'd make it a point to stop in on Isabelle and her husband.

"Anyway, ask one of the nurses and I'm sure they'll know the room number," she replies. "Just ask for Frank Sands."

"Mr. Sands?"

"Yes."

"Not Mr. Sands, *Mister Sands*?" I repeat, wanting to add, *My* Mr. Sands? *The man who never even once told me he had a wife?!* Yes, okay, he'd spoken of having a wife, just like I'd spoken of having a father. But I'd assumed she was out of the picture too. *Where has she been all this time?*

"Unless there's someone else here by the same name," she replies with a laugh. "You seem surprised. Did Frank tell you he was single so he could woo you?"

"No! He just doesn't talk about you a lot." This gets an even bigger laugh from the woman standing in front of me. "I mean—"

"Don't apologize, this sounds very much like my Frank. You know what, Grace? I was just on my way out, but I think you and I should walk into his room together and we'll let him explain himself. Come," she commands, wriggling her arm through mine and leading me down the hall.

When we're a few feet from Mr. Sands's room, Mrs. Sands stops. "Grace, you know Frank hasn't been doing well recently," she says, and I nod. "I don't know when

59

you last saw him, but I just don't want his condition to come as a shock to you when we go inside."

"Thanks," I reply, realizing Mrs. Sands must have no idea how frequently I visit her husband. "But I don't think I'll be too surprised."

And yet when we walk in and I see Mr. Sands lying on his bed in his pj's, his eyes closed, an oxygen tank pumping air through a tube connected to his nose, the wind gets knocked out of me yet again.

"Frank Sands, are you sleeping or are you just playing possum?" Mrs. Sands says in a loud, clear voice.

The muscles of Mr. Sands's cheeks pull slightly in the direction of a smile as his eyelids slowly open. Mrs. Sands moves us both closer to the bed, and when Mr. Sands registers that she and I are standing there together, he's the one who looks surprised.

"Oh boy," he says, his reply actually sounding somewhat boyish despite the hoarseness of his voice.

"That's right," she replies. "Grace and I had to meet in the bathroom, no thanks to you. And do you know what this lovely young lady told me? She said you'd told her you didn't have a wife."

"No! I never said that!" I answer, not knowing whom I'm supposed to address. "I just said you never mentioned her." I look between Mr. and Mrs. Sands and realize that didn't come out exactly as intended either. "Tell her!" I say to Mr. Sands pleadingly.

"Okay, okay," he replies slowly, accompanied by a

half chuckle, half wheeze. "This is hard for me to say, but Isabelle, Gracie and I are running away together. We would have told you sooner, but we needed to secure the passports first."

I turn to Mrs. Sands, who doesn't look entirely amused. "That's not true."

"Well," she replies, "I'm on to you both now. And if I weren't so distracted by all the attention I'm getting from Victor, the young handyman who comes to help me change lightbulbs, I might be very upset."

"Oh, there, there, Iz," Mr. Sands interjects. "I'm sure Grace would be willing to share me."

I nod, knowing they're joking with each other, but feeling a bizarre tension in the room nonetheless.

"Well then, Grace, I'll leave him to you now since I've already had my time with our man here," she says, keeping her eyes on Mr. Sands. "You'll be okay, Frank?"

"Thank you, honey," he replies, and strains to reach out to her. Mrs. Sands sees this too, and wraps her hand around his arm, giving it a good squeeze as she smiles down at him.

"Good." She turns to me. "Grace, it was lovely to meet you at long last. And now I understand why my husband here wanted to keep us apart. He probably suspected if I saw how fetching you were, I would insist on a chaperone for your visits."

"It was nice meeting you, Mrs. Sands," I reply, forcing a smile. She smiles back, winks at her husband, then turns to go. After she passes through the door, I turn back to Mr. Sands. "You never—"

"I know."

"Because I thought—"

"I know," he repeats, cutting me off again. "I wanted you to think that."

"Huh?" I take a step back from the bed.

"Do you have any idea what it's like to be here, Grace?"

"Um, well . . . no."

"Can you imagine how miserable it would be to have your world shrink to the size of a hospital bed?"

I shake my head.

Mr. Sands closes his eyes and continues. "It's not like my life was some big, grand thing, or that I was a terribly powerful or important man," he says, reopening his eyes and finding mine. "But I loved my life, Grace. I loved getting up at five forty-five every morning and going to work. I loved building my business from nothing into something. I loved the idea that I was making decisions that mattered. Spending time with my little girls and watching them grow into strong-willed, independent women. Loved that I had a hand in shaping them. I was active in the community. In local politics. I played sports. I went to games, and the movies and concerts. I never did much traveling, but I always imagined I would. And now, look at this. Look at me! All I have is this bed, and the only place I go is into that wheelchair—and the goddamn solarium if I'm lucky! Can you imagine living like this?"

"Mr. Sands," I say softly.

"I know it was juvenile of me not to have introduced you to Isabelle earlier, but I have no independence or privacy anymore. I'm an adult—and yet I can't do anything by myself at this point. I don't have the strength to open a bottle of pills on my own," he says, sadness and anger making the rasp of his voice sound even huskier. "For Christ's sake, I can't even go to the bathroom without having someone help me. So if I tried to have a friendship with you separate from the one I have with my wife and with all the other people around here who have to wipe my nose and my ass for me, it's because spending time with you alone has let me feel like . . . like a person again. I even flatter myself to think that maybe you've even come to see me as a father figure of sorts. Do you know how important that is to me? To feel useful to someone?"

I nod, not sure of what to say, but getting it.

"So that's why I never particularly wanted you and Isabelle to meet, Grace. I just wanted to feel like I had some privacy. Some sense of dignity as a man. Can you appreciate that?"

"Sure," I say, thinking about the word *dignity,* and knowing how important the concept is to Mr. Sands. Whenever we spoke about his adventures in the Marine Corps, he'd always talk about the significance of doing one's duty as a soldier while "acting with dignity." It wasn't just some abstract notion or random rule to him. To Mr. Sands, having dignity meant consciously choosing the way you wanted to live, and possessing the character required to make those decisions for yourself. "Is that why you asked *me* to help you instead of asking her?"

"Please, Grace," he replies, "I still feel terrible about that. I should never have asked you. It was a low moment, to say the least." Mr. Sands's eyes close. "Please let's not speak of it again, okay?" He's exhausted, that's clear.

"I'm going to let you rest," I say, and he gives a quiet moan of response. I keep my eyes on him as I back out of the room. Though it's not an official rule, I know the staff prefers the doors on this hallway to remain open. But I want to give Mr. Sands the privacy and dignity he deserves, so I close the door behind me.

It's not much, but it's all I can think to do to help him right now.

⟁ ⟁ ⟁

I need to focus on something new. A change of scenery. A drastic modification. If a person's aura has a particular color, what I'm looking for is something to help me get to the other side of the rainbow. But right now the selection of a new hair color at the Fulton Pharmacy is going to have to suffice. As I walk there from Hanover House I try to reassure myself that like the ads promise, a new hue will give me "a whole new outlook!"

Before heading to the hair care section, I pick up a sour apple Blow Pop from the front stand and stick it behind my ear flower-style to keep both hands free for box comparison purposes. Maybe I was born to be a golden blonde but got colored by the wrong cosmic crayon? I glance at the rounded shoplifter mirror that hangs above the shelf to see if I can envision myself as "Platinum Ice," but instead of seeing myself, the image I see reflected in the mirror is Lolly's boyfriend, Jake.

Normally seeing Jake wouldn't particularly bother me. Sure, he's a turd, but usually he's a turd easily sidestepped. Not today. Right now I can't seem to take my eyes off him in that mirror because Jake is standing there kissing a girl.

A girl who is not my sister.

This is not good. And, even worse, the girl Jake is kissing happens to be Natalie Talbot. The girl from Milk Bar. Pretty Natalie Talbot. Popular Natalie Talbot. Everybody loves Natalie Talbot. I'm barely blinking as I stare slack-jawed into that mirror. Jake's got his hand around her waist and he's moving it up and down. The only thought that occurs to me in the moment is "Run!" because the last thing I want to do is be seen by that two-timing dipwad mid-two-time. I put the hair dye box back on the shelf without making any sudden movements, then head for the door. I don't look back, I just keep my eyes on the parking lot ahead of me, and finally exhale when I arrive at the second row of parked cars. As I comb my hands through my hair, the sour apple Blow Pop drops from behind my ear and falls onto the asphalt.

Oh, dammit!

I pick up the wrapped lollipop and realize I've technically just stolen it. I've done a lot of stupid things in my day, but this is officially the first thing I've lifted. People *intentionally* shoplift all the time. This was a total mistake. It's a twenty-five- to fifty-cent mistake at most, and I know it's not that big a deal . . . yet I also know that if I don't go back and give the cashier the money, I'll obsess about it later. I'll worry that any good karma I've built up will be erased, and my prayers will be dismissed for the price of a Blow Pop.

I walk back into the store. *Grace, don't let your eyes wander, just keep staring at the woman behind the register.*

Thankfully there's no one in line ahead of me, so I set the lollipop down on the counter. "I accidentally walked out of the store without paying," I explain, digging a quarter out of my pocket and holding it out to her. "But it was a mistake, I swear."

"What is this, a joke?" the cashier asks.

"No, I just—" I start to say, then realize it's not worth it. I just need to get out before Jake and Natalie spot me. But when I hear two aluminum cans being set down on the counter behind me, I know it's game over. I turn around.

"Hi, Jake," I say, pronouncing his name as if I were saying the word *fuckface.*

"Oh, hey." He nods trying to look casual as he slides both energy drinks closer toward him. "Blow Pop, huh?"

If he makes a joke about me practicing blow jobs on the Blow Pop—and seriously, he has that kind of sense of humor—I might "accidentally" pop him in the nuts.

"Yeah," I reply.

"Sour apple." Natalie nods, stepping out from behind Jake to take a look. "Those are my favorite too. Hey, Grace." She smiles.

Hey, Grace? Natalie Talbot knows my name?

"Sour apple is so much better than watermelon," she adds. And she's right. I wonder if she also knows my sister is dating the bonehead she was just kissing.

I nod.

"Oh, man, Jake, you should have seen the last project Grace did in our art class. It was so funny, it was this collage of celebrity faces framed by a border of words, from articles about their scandals," Natalie says, pulling at the sleeve of his shirt.

"Cool, maybe you can show it to me sometime," he says with a smile. *If he thinks that's enough to buy me off, he's sadly mistaken.* When Jake gets his change back from the cashier, he turns to Natalie. "We should go."

"Okay." She smiles again. "See ya, Grace."

"Later, G.M." Jake nods.

I am completely stunned. I wait for them to get into Jake's Mustang before I walk out of the store myself. I'm already composing the conversation with Eric in my head. He's going to love this. I look at my watch and assume practice will probably be over, so I grab my cell and call his home number.

"Hello?" Mrs. Ward says when she picks up.

"Hi, Mrs. Ward, it's Grace."

"Hey, honey! Oh, you just missed Eric. He got back from practice, hit the shower, then said he was going to be meeting up with some friends at Milk Bar."

Part of me wants to ask Mrs. Ward who these friends are, but a bigger part of me doesn't really want to know. Or is scared to. "Oh, right," I reply instead. "Milk Bar."

"I'm sure if you head over there now you'll catch them."

"Yeah, okay, thanks. Bye, Mrs. Ward."

"Bye, Grace."

I know it's stupid to be mad that Eric is going to "our" coffee shop with other people, and yet I can't deny the twinge I feel. I unwrap my Blow Pop and jam it into my mouth. But not even a sour apple lollipop tastes good to me now. So when I pass the first trash can I see, I chuck it and hear the candy shatter as it hits the bottom of the pail.

Chapter Seven

As soon as I open the front door to Hanover House on Tuesday afternoon, Patty Ray gives me the royal welcome.

"Grace!" she yells down the hall. "How are we today?"

"We're good, thanks. How are you?"

"I am regretting that my lunch salad contained both onions and asparagus," Patty replies, fanning her hand in front of her mouth. "I stink from every direction! T.M.I., I know, just can't help myself," she says cheerfully. "And I have a special message for you."

"You do?" I ask, keeping my distance as I try to remain outside the smell zone.

"Jeff wants you to drop by his office when you get a chance."

"Really? Why?"

Patty shakes her head. "Well, I don't really know . . . but it might have something to do with that nice couple the Sandses." This woman knows everything. I'm tempted to press her on the subject, but I'd rather not run Mr. Sands's business through the gossip channels myself if I can help it.

When I knock at his office door, Jeff waves me in. "Grace, come, sit," he says, motioning to the little couch to the side of the room. Once I take my seat he stands, closes the office door, then sits next to me.

"Heard you met Isabelle Sands the other day. She's quite a character, isn't she?" He shakes his head and smiles.

"She seems nice, I guess," I say, already wondering if she's asked him to tell me I should stop visiting Mr. Sands so much.

"Well good, I'm glad you think so, because I'd like you to start spending some time with her when you're here too."

"But . . ." *What? No!* "Why?" I say as coolly as I can.

"I've worked here quite a while now, Grace, and I've found that there are just a few illnesses that are harder to deal with than others. I think Lou Gehrig's disease is one of them, not only because of the way it debilitates the sufferer, but because of the toll on the person's family too. That's why if I can find a way to make the caregiver's life a little better, I try to."

"Okay . . . but why do you want me to visit with Mrs. Sands?"

"Because, Grace," Jeff says, smiling and shaking his head, "I think you'd help make her life better."

"No, but really, why?"

"I am completely serious." He laughs. "I'm sure she'd like your company and I think you'd be a real lifeline to her. That's why I'm asking you to embrace the friction."

"*Huh?*" I recoil.

"Warrior slang." Jeff nods. "When a commanding officer tells his troops to 'embrace the friction' or 'embrace the suck,' he's saying that he understands the situation he's sending them into is tough, but he needs them to march forward and do their jobs anyway."

I bite my lip. Ordinarily, spending time with a resident who's healthy and happy to take care of herself is the kind of assignment everyone here wants. Basically those are the people who don't want you to do anything for them. They see it as a point of pride to do everything themselves, so you wind up doing way less than you're supposed to. Play your cards right and they even bake stuff for you. But especially after my last conversation with Mr. Sands, I don't want to be disloyal to him. I don't want him to think I'm "cheating" on him. Especially not with his wife.

"Well, when I met her she seemed like she was handling things pretty well. And I'll bet she's the kind of woman who has tons of friends around here. So I'm sure she wouldn't want someone like *me* hanging around and bothering her."

"Grace, I think you'll be able to give her a certain amount of comfort that no one else here can."

"How?"

"Go to her, Grace, talk to her."

"About what?" I shrug with great exaggeration.

Jeff gives one of his easy smiles. "About anything you want. Whatever feels right. Okay?"

"I'm not sure—"

"I'm not asking you to clean bedpans, Grace." And with that, Jeff rises and points me to the door. "I think you'll find Mrs. Sands in her unit on Jane Lane right now. You know, you're earning some serious karma points here."

"Great," I say as I leave the office wondering if she knows that her husband had slipped me an envelope of pills. "I'm sure I can use them."

♫ ♫ ♫

I walk out of the main building of Hanover House and head for the cottages. There's definitely a different feeling around these little places than in the main building. They're built to look like bungalows, and they'd be a cool place to live—if only they weren't on the grounds of a retirement community. I look up to the sky, which is a beautiful shade of blue and full of cotton-ball clouds. *What is the point to this? And what exactly am I supposed to do here?* Though I asked Jeff similar questions, I wasn't satisfied (or happy) with his answers. And even though no further response seems to be coming, I still can't help asking another: *Why me?*

The Sandses' cottage has a cheerful exterior and there are marigolds growing in the window boxes. It almost looks like one of those houses on a postcard, with a big American flag waving out front, suggesting that good, solid citizens live here. The front door is open, so I knock on the side of the screen door, but there's no response. I can hear the TV on in the background so I'm pretty sure Mrs. Sands is home. But when I knock again, more loudly this time, still no answer.

"Hello?" I call out.

Nothing.

"It's Grace Manning," I say. I wait for another minute. "Hello?" When I don't get a response, suddenly I'm a little worried, so I open the screen door and walk in. The entry that leads to the main living room area is dark, but there are pictures of Mr. and Mrs. Sands on the front table. I bend forward to get a better look, and I see a picture of Mrs. Sands, with a ridiculously high hairdo, a sleeveless blouse, capri pants, and Keds sitting on top of a llama and smiling widely, as if she's completely aware of how ridiculous she looks but is having so much fun, she doesn't care. Next to it, there's a photo of Mr. and Mrs. Sands standing in front of some incredibly ornate temple, the kind I always picture when I think of Thailand—probably because I've seen images like this on the front of the local Thai restaurant's takeout menu. On the other side of that, there's a picture of a little boy who looks about five years old, standing in seersucker short pants and a little bow tie with a pained expression on his face. He's dressed like it's the 1920s or something, but from the digital date stamp on the side, you can tell that it was only taken eleven years ago, making the kid about my age.

When I look up, my eyes having finally adjusted to the darkness, I see a figure sitting on the couch in the living room, staring blankly in the direction of the television.

"Mrs. Sands?" I walk toward her.

At this, she finally turns and looks at me. She smiles slightly, but it's more one of those dazed *who are you and what the hell are you doing in my living room?* kind of expressions. I'm wondering the same thing myself.

"Hi," I say, wanting to follow up with "And bye!"

"Oh. Hello," she replies in a tone that suggests she's not sure who I am.

"Grace." I point to myself and nod.

"Yes." Mrs. Sands nods her head. "I recall." She quickly brushes her index fingers under her eyes, then drops her hands back to her sides. It's the same gesture I use when I'm watching a stupid movie—or worse, a sappy commercial—that makes my eyes leak. Especially if I'm with Eric and I don't want him to see that I'm crying, I try to make it look like I'm just adjusting any eyeliner that's smearing down my face. But when another fat teardrop drips off Mrs. Sands's eyelash, she just shakes her head, realizing it's no use. "Forgive me." She puts both hands in front of her eyes. "I've never understood those people who say a good cry can make you feel better. Crying just makes me feel worse." She shakes her head. "And it'll prematurely wrinkle your eyes, so you should be careful."

"I'll try."

"These days, I can't seem to help myself, though," she says, as if chastising herself. I look to the wall clock and try to figure how long I need to spend here before I can flee. Mrs. Sands wipes her nose and looks back to me. "I've started carrying extra tissues wherever I go. I practically have a whole tissue box shoved up my sleeve." She waves her wrist in the air and there is a bulge right under her cuff. "At least when I used to shove tissues in my shirt, I'd distribute them to better places." She points to her chest, and I see a smile forming on her lips. "Good thing they didn't have those water bras in my day. With my luck the darned thing would have sprung a leak, and I would have wound up with papier-mâché breasts."

"Never thought of that," I say with a laugh.

"Hey, you gotta be careful—" Mrs. Sands warns, a note of mock seriousness entering her voice, "or the smile lines will get you too."

"Yeah, my mom calls her wrinkles smile lines, but she doesn't smile enough to have earned all those creases in her face."

"That's a terrible thing to say, Grace," Mrs. Sands responds, "and I'm beginning to understand why my husband likes you so much! Come, sit." She beckons me to the couch. "You know I still can't believe it took us this long to finally meet."

"I know." I try to make myself comfortable on the cushion farthest away from her. "I'm just surprised we didn't bump into each other sooner."

"Well, I think by the time you arrive in the late afternoons, Frank has already kicked me out for the day. I spend mornings over there when you're at school, I suppose. Then at a certain point after lunch every day, he shoos me away. 'Get out, Izzy! Do some of the fancy activities they have here, do some exercise,' he says." Mrs. Sands laughs. "Exercise, honestly! Never enjoyed it as a young woman, don't think that's really going to change at this age."

"I hear you."

She laughs again. "We run through this same routine every day. Silly, I know, but I think it makes both of us feel better. Oh, Grace, where are my manners? Can I get you something to drink?" Standing, Mrs. Sands looks livelier, more like she'd seemed the other day. "Maybe a Pepsi?" she suggests. "I have to warn you, though, I only have the caffeine-free stuff."

"Oh, that's okay," I reply, thinking that though I could explain to Mr. Sands that I came here because it was a job requirement, part of me doesn't want him to think I might enjoy it.

"Well, I'm not much of a fan of the caffeine-free stuff, myself—if you can't enjoy the buzz, why bother?—but my doctor seems to feel I get enough of it in the coffee I drink. Six cups a day," she whispers. "No way he'll get me to give that up. He'll have to pry the Folgers out of my cold dead hands."

Mrs. Sands then reaches into the freezer and takes out one of those old-fashioned 1950s ice trays. The metal kind with the handle you pull to help the ice cubes come out without making you have to bang the tray against the counter. "I mean what's the point of living if you take all the little pleasures away, right? Speaking of . . ." She opens a cabinet, pulls out a bag of those giant Pepperidge Farm chocolate chunk cookies, and holds it out for me to take over to the coffee table. "Only live once, right?"

"Sure, thanks." I nod as Mrs. Sands takes two glasses down from the cabinet, puts a few ice cubes in each, then pours out the can of soda, half in each glass.

"So tell me, Grace." She hands me the glass. "Why are you working in an awful place like this?"

"It's not that bad." I shrug. I want to tell her that I actually enjoy spending time with her husband, but I don't want to sound like a suck-up. Instead, I just open the white Pepperidge Farm bag and take out an over-sized cookie.

"Oh, please!" exclaims Mrs. Sands. "I had a job I hated when I was your age too. I worked the cash register in my father's grocery store. Oh, it was so miserable. I wanted to quit every day, but when your dad's your boss—"

"You're screwed." I take a bite of the cookie and sink my teeth right into a chunk of chip. The bittersweet chocolate makes me feel better almost immediately.

"Exactly," she laughs, plucking a cookie from the bag. "It was the worst. All the popular girls used to come into the store and they'd seem so care-free, so lucky. And I'd feel so, well, stuck."

"But now you're going to tell me that those were their glory days and they're never as popular again as they were in high school, right?"

"Ah . . . no." Mrs. Sands smiles. "You're not stupid, Grace," she says. "Those girls almost always find a way to get what they want. *But*," she says with emphasis, "I promise they do become less important in your life until eventually they don't matter at all. Popularity, like being really rich, isn't always as much fun as it seems. I've seen enough of both cases to know that's true."

"Yeah, well, I wouldn't mind giving either one a shot for a day or two." I envision myself standing through the sunroof of a limousine waving to passersby, a tiara affixed to my perfectly styled hair, which, though blowing in the breeze, miraculously avoids getting stuck to my lip gloss.

Mrs. Sands nods. "I know what you mean, but be careful what you're wishing for. I've also learned that the man upstairs can have a very wicked sense of humor."

No kidding.

"So you have daughters, right?" I ask, swirling the ice cubes in my drink.

"Two," Mrs. Sands replies. "What about you, any kids?"

"None that I'm aware of."

"Good," she laughs, "just checking. What about siblings?"

"Yeah, I have an older sister, Lolly."

"Lolly? Short for Lorraine?"

"Yep, but nobody ever gets that," I tell her. "Actually, she won't admit it anymore, but she's known as Lolly because of me. I couldn't pronounce the name Lorraine when I was a kid, and just used to say 'Lolly,' which stuck."

"Do you two get along?"

"Er, mostly," I say. "She's just really into being her boyfriend's girlfriend right now."

"I see." She nods.

"She's always trying to impress him, laughs at everything he says. And trust me, he's *really* not that funny."

"Sisterhood isn't easy," Mrs. Sands replies. "It's supposed to be the most natural thing in the world, and yet an overabundance of estrogen can really screw things up."

"Yeah, at my house it's just my sister, my mother, and me now, so we've got a lot of that going around."

"Well." Mrs. Sands wipes the bottom of her perspiring glass on her pants before setting it down on the coffee table. "Please know that if you ever need a break, you are more than welcome here. And," she continues, sticking her index finger in the air, "I promise I'll keep out of your way. You can sit, watch TV, talk if you want, or not talk if you don't want to, and I'll respect that."

"Thanks." I believe she really would do just that. "That's really nice of you."

"Nonsense," she replies. "It's not nice of me at all. I say this for purely selfish reasons. See, you coming here and spending time with me will make all the rest of the crabby old ladies in this place very jealous!"

"Thank you."

"Well, I don't want to keep you now, I'm sure you have other tasks you're supposed to accomplish before you can get out of here."

My head bobs from side to side. I'm not sure if this is her cue or mine, but I think I probably have spent enough time here today to satisfy everyone, so I stand. "I'm back in on Thursday, so I'm sure I'll see you then."

"Oh, and hang on a second, Grace." Mrs. Sands stands up and walks over to her purse, which is sitting on the kitchen chair. She reaches into her wallet and pulls out a twenty-dollar bill. "Take this," she says, handing me the cash.

I eye the money suspiciously, wanting to take it from her, but not sure if I should. "What's it for?"

"It's for nothing. It's because I want you to have it."

"Oh, no, Mrs. Sands I really couldn't," I protest, shaking my head but still wanting the money. "I get paid to work here, so—"

"So I'm sure they're not paying you enough and it's always nice to have a little extra," she says with a wink.

"But . . ."

"Please, Grace, you're such a breath of fresh air in this dreary place—and you've really been going above and beyond the call of duty helping Frank—so I want you to have it. Buy something fun for yourself." She folds my hand over the bill, then pats it, signaling the discussion is closed.

When I leave the cottage, I head back to the main building to drop in on Mr. Sands. His door is closed again, but before my knuckles connect with the door, my hand drops back to my side. Part of me is scared that Mr. Sands will be mad when he hears I spent time with his wife. Then there's the other part: the part that's worried that if I knock, a new nurse will come to the door and tell me his condition has gotten worse. What Jeff said about this disease taking an extra toll on the patient's family runs through my head. The not knowing, day to day, if this will be the visit I find him unable to move, breathe, chew, or talk, makes me anxious. Makes me wonder how much he's suffering. *If there's anything I can do to relieve that suffering.* And it makes me feel pretty horrible to admit that what I'm hoping for now is that his suffering won't last very long . . .

The more I think about it, the more uneasy I get. I can't go in. But as I turn and walk away from Mr. Sands's door, the nerves are replaced by the hollow feeling. It's not that I think a visit from me could make anything better for Mr. Sands, it's more that I'd like to be able to help and yet feel totally useless.

♪ ♪ ♪

"Don't!" Lolly yells from upstairs as I turn on the TV in the living room.

"What?" I yell back, flipping through the channels and sitting down on the couch.

"I was just going to watch my soap," she says, coming down the stairs with the remote in her hand.

"You have it recorded, you can watch it anytime."

"I don't care," Lolly replies, shaking her head and waggling her finger back and forth.

"You look like Mom when you do that."

"No, I don't!" Lolly yells, stopping her finger mid-wag. I look at my sister standing there in that white V-neck undershirt, cut-off army pants, her hair knotted in a fat bun at the top of her head, and all I can think about is that Jake is cheating on her. "And move, 'cause I want to lay on the couch. Seriously, Grace, my back is killing me and I have cramps," Lolly says, throwing down the period card.

The period card is like the Joker—it's one of those wild cards that signals to the other player, *"You have been warned: I can't be held accountable for my behavior if you disturb me now."* If I had been considering telling Lolly about Jake and what I'd seen at the pharmacy the other day, I know now is definitely *not* the right time to do it. Not that there really is a *right* time to learn about that kind of stuff. There definitely wasn't a right mood for Mom when she found out Dad had actually left for another woman.

After he split but before Mom heard someone else was in the picture, I'm pretty sure Mom also believed Dad would come back and things would work out again. Yeah, she was pissed that Dad had just disappeared, but I think part of her held on to the idea that nothing was keeping him from reappearing in the same way. We all did. Once she got the news about Nancy Falton, the prayer leader at the church, though—the news that Nancy had been subbed in as her replacement—that was the kicker. Mom had run into Tina Cordell, a teacher in the church's preschool and one of Nancy's best friends, at the grocery store three days after he left, and Tina had casually asked Mom how she was doing "now that Daniel's moved in with Nancy." I don't know how Mom reacted in the supermarket, but by the time she got home, she had completely lost it. The rest of the night she raged. "Even if that scumbag father of yours dares to come crawling back," she yelled, "even if he admits what a stupid mistake he made, there's no way. There's no way I'd let him come back. I have too much pride for that." Lolly and I just kind of sat there on the couch, not knowing if we were supposed to turn the TV off or sit there without moving until she stopped howling and the storm passed.

Mom ranted on for a while and kept talking about *pride* this and *pride* that. But that was the part that made the least sense to me because pride's one of those tricky things. Sometimes people tell you it's good; you want to have it in the "I'm proud of you, son," or "I'm proud to be an American" way. They tie it up with a sense of honor, self-esteem, and a lot of times with dignity. But there's a difference. Unlike dignity, sometimes having too much pride is completely negative: It's one of the seven deadly sins—the thing that'll get you in the end and cause your demise. So when Mom said she had too much pride to let Dad come back (*if he ever tried to*), I couldn't decide if that was the good pride or bad pride because in a weird way, it seemed like both.

I look at Lolly standing above me on the couch, and I'm certain neither one of us is up to the "guess what I saw?" chat right now, even if it does seem like her pride could stand to be taken down a few notches. So I just shake my head and get up, surrendering the couch. I head upstairs to my room and close the door. Kicking my shoes off, I lie down on my bed and stare up at the ceiling.

"Me again," I say somewhat loudly, as if trying to wake a sleeping giant. Maybe he has been asleep at the wheel, since *nothing* has gotten better since I last prayed. *"Okay, I'm going to assume you can hear me, even if I speak a little softer,"* I continue, shifting my eyes back up to the ceiling. *"I've got a couple of new questions for you today."* I'm trying to decide where to start, putting my list in the right order of importance, but my mouth is running again before I think the whole thing through. *"Dad. I need a little help understanding him. When is he coming back? And how could you let him run away in the first place?"* I barely get that question out of my mouth before I'm on to the next one, anger quickly building and crashing over me. *"Okay, speaking of stuff that shouldn't be happening, let's talk again about Mr. Sands. I mean, why would you give him such a horrible disease? Why? He doesn't deserve this."* The next thought dawns as quickly as the last. *"And tell me this: Lolly. Why so bitchy?"* I exhale and stare hard at the ceiling.

But there's no reply.

And there's no movement.

No nothing.

The only thing I feel now is the heat radiating in my cheeks because the rest of me feels empty. My hands are cold, and as I bring them to my face to try to cool it down, I hear the doorbell ring downstairs.

"Grace!" Lolly yells.

I don't reply.

"Grace!" she shouts again. "Your BOYFRIEND's here!"

My what? Who? Oh, no, she must mean Eric . . . She didn't just say that right in front of him! *What is wrong with that girl?!*

I run down the stairs and pull Eric away from Lolly as quickly as I can, mouthing "bite me" to my sister as she saunters back to the couch. "Sorry about that," I say with a wince when Eric and I get outside.

"Your sister," Eric replies, zipping and unzipping his Windbreaker, a new jacket emblazoned with our school's name on the back. "She's a piece of work, huh?"

"She's a piece of something, that's for sure. What's up?"

"Will you take a ride with me over to the mall? I need a dress shirt." When Eric sees my raised eyebrow, he adds, "I'm worried if I go with my mom, I'll wind up with some weird collarless, ruffled thing."

"Maybe ruffles are what have been missing in your life," I reply.

Eric smiles and shakes his head as he taps up the kickstand of my bike and rolls it to me, squeezing Big Blue's sparkly banana seat. "Great, I completely forgot who I was talking to."

"You're just jealous you don't have anything so spiff on your bike, mister. But if you're lucky, maybe we can find you a shirt with ruffles *and* sparkles." I snatch my bike from his hands. "And by the way, you are so going to lose this race." I hop on the bike and start sprinting down the street.

"We'll see about that," shouts Eric, grabbing his bike, which he'd ditched on the lawn, and chasing after me.

I pedal as hard and as fast as I can, but by the second block, Eric overtakes me. "Let you win," I say, out of breath as he passes me.

He slows to my pace. "Yeah, I figured. You were just trying to build my confidence, right?"

"That's right." I massage the stabbing pain in my right side. "When did you get those wings put on your wheels?"

"I'm telling you, Grace," Eric says as we both start to coast, "the coach kills me at practice. Works me so hard that by the end I don't know whether I'm going to puke or cry, and sometimes I do both. But I think it's paying off. I just feel stronger, and look . . ." Eric takes his right leg off the pedal and when he flexes his calf, a double muscle appears; on top of the long calf muscle running down the back of his leg is another shorter but pronounced one.

I whistle, surprised and impressed, which makes both of us laugh since I have a feeling Eric probably feels the same way. I also know this isn't the kind of display Eric goes around doing, but he showed me because that's the kind of thing you can share with your best friend and nobody else.

"Keep that up and we won't be able to find any clothes to fit you there, Popeye."

"You know, that's a risk I'm willing to take." Eric smiles, a little embarrassed.

When we get into the mall, I direct him to the one guy's store I know, R. T. Smith's, since I figure it should be safe, ruffle-free terrain. As I wade through the displays, I spot a sales rack jammed with dress shirts. "Bingo," I say, pulling two shirts off the rack and holding them up against Eric.

Eric shakes his head. "Grace, those are XXLs. Now, I know I probably come across as large and in charge, but I don't think I'm quite there yet." Hard to deny; the shirts are long enough to be dresses on him.

Though I've never been much of a shopper myself, I know Eric's relying on me, so I do my best to fake it. "Life's a con game," Mr. Sands once told me. "Act confident and people will assume you are." I pick out a few shirts and motion Eric back to the dressing room area. Eric trails behind me, seeming entirely content that I've taken the lead on this.

"You'll be okay in there by yourself?" I tease.

"I hope so," he says, entering the dressing room.

I stand close to the door and unintentionally catch a glimpse of him through the slats as he's changing. I should probably move farther away, but I don't. "So," I say, leaning a little closer to the door, "you are not going to believe what I saw at the pharmacy the other day."

"Tell me."

"Okay, there I am picking up a few things when I spy Lolly's boyfriend, Jake, making out with Natalie Talbot in the back of the store."

"Jake and Natalie Talbot?" Eric repeats, coming out of the dressing room as if he heard wrong. "Hot Natalie?"

"The very one." I nod, giving Eric the once-over. I shake my head at the shirt. "The shoulders aren't quite right."

Eric nods in agreement and heads back into the dressing room. "So Jake and Natalie?" he says again, like he's mulling the information, then decides there's no possible chance this could be true. Like I've just told him that I cloned his cat. "How would a poser like Jake score someone as gorgeous as her?"

"Well, she's *okay*." I never knew Eric had given so much thought to Natalie.

"Grace, she's by far the prettiest girl in the whole school. By. Far."

"Yeah, well." I'm sorry I brought it up.

A moment later he opens the door and comes out in another shirt. "I know why she wouldn't want to date Rich anymore—he's the definition of d-bag—but why would someone that hot be interested in *Jake*? Natalie could have anyone she wants. I mean, that's just stupid!" He slaps his palm against his forehead as if he's disappointed in her for making such a poor choice.

"Okay, I get it," I snap, jamming my hands into the back pocket of my jeans. "You think Natalie's pretty."

"Ye-ah," he says, making it a two-syllable word and smiling widely. "So what do you think?" He motions to the shirt.

"Eh." I shrug my shoulders, sending Eric back into the dressing room. "Well *anyway*, the reason I told you is because I have to decide when and if I should tell Lolly. I mean, maybe she'd just be better off not knowing, if it was just a one-time thing, you know? On the one hand it's probably better if she finds out sooner rather than later and at home instead of in school, right? But on the other, do I really want to get in the middle of all this? I mean, it just doesn't seem like there's a really good outcome here whatever happens. So what do you think I should do?"

"No idea," he replies through the door. Of course he has no idea, he's probably still thinking about Natalie. "Damn, there are so many buttons on this thing. Anyway, Lolly probably already knows on some level, don't you think?"

"I'm not so sure." I think about the conversation I had with Mr. Sands and our mutual *ignore the problem, make it go away* strategy. It's as if that expression "We see what we want to see" is a survival technique used by all people in every circumstance.

When Eric comes out of the dressing room this time, he's in a light blue shirt that matches his eyes perfectly.

The fit is just right too. He looks great. Really, really great.

"Yeah, that's the one." I nod.

"Good." He smiles. "It was my favorite too, which is why I saved it for last. *So,*" he says, "don't you even want to know why I need a dress shirt?"

"Oh, yeah, why?"

"Well, you know that spring dance they're going to be having? I was thinking it could really suck *or*, it might actually be fun. I've kind of been on the fence about it."

"Well, now that you mention it, yeah, I feel the same way." I also feel the inside of my stomach starting to gallop.

"And I thought it'd be more fun if we went together. *Sooo,* do you want to go with me?" In the millisecond the question hangs there and before I can even respond, Eric rushes in to fill the silence. "I mean, I don't know," he says, glancing away. "Mike said it'd probably a good idea to go because a lot of the upperclassmen on the team are going to be there, and he thinks it's important for bonding or whatever."

"Oh," I reply as this extra piece of information filters through brain and body, "you want me to go with you to the school dance so you can bond with the guys on the basketball team?"

"Well," says Eric, *instead of saying no.*

The thing in my stomach that had been galloping just a moment ago slams into a wood jump, knocks over the poles, and throws the rider. *I'm an idiot!* "I'll think about it, okay?"

"What do you have to think about?" Eric replies. "I mean, go or not, whatever, it's no big deal."

"No, I know, it's just—"

"Well, let me know," he says as he walks back into the dressing room.

As I stand there on the other side of the door, I bite my lower lip hard. Why didn't I just say yes? Why *did* I make such a big deal? It's Eric. And I blew it. I roll my eyes skyward. *"Can you tell me at what age a person stops making mistakes like this?"*

No answer.

No surprise.

Chapter Eight

"So what would you do?" I ask. "What's the right answer, Mrs. Sands?"

"Grace, what I would do and what the right answer is, well . . ." She laughs. "Those are likely two different responses. And please, call me by my first name. None of this 'missus' stuff, got it?"

We're sitting on the step of her front porch. I had no intention of telling her about what had happened between Eric and me—and I had no intention of coming back here before I saw Mr. Sands again either—but I did. And it all just started spilling out as we shared a bowl of ice cream and Isabelle asked if I had anyone "special" in my life.

"Well, there's this guy at school, he's my best friend," I tell her. "It's not like he's my boyfriend or anything like that . . ."

"But you want him to be?" When I don't respond right away, Isabelle adds, "Or you're not really sure what you want?"

I shrug. "I don't think he thinks of me like that," I say, recalling the way my stomach ached after he explained the real reason he wanted to go to that stupid dance with me. "Anyway, from what I can tell, nothing good ever comes from relationships like that. I mean, they just seem to lead to problems—one person always winds up disappointing the other person—and then you break up, and in the end you hate the person you'd liked the most. So it's probably best if Eric and I don't screw up what we have."

"I can see why you might not want him to become your boyfriend when you put it like that." Isabelle licks her spoon and her thoughts seem to drift for a moment. "Nothing wrong with that, though." She nods.

That's when I ask her what she would do, whether she would accept an invitation to the dance that came thanks to Mike Richter's instruction.

"Well, I'm no relationship expert, and don't let anyone fool you, Grace: No one's an 'expert' at such things even if they've had hundreds of relationships themselves. And what can those people really tell you anyway?"

"How to treat an STD?"

"Precisely!" Isabelle replies. "*But,* when I first started dating Frank, I was so scared it wasn't going to work out between us, the way I acted, it was almost as if I were trying to push him away."

"So you were friends before you started dating?" I ask, feeling a little weird as soon as the question comes out of my mouth. Somehow the idea of discussing Mr. Sands's life behind his back seems wrong . . . even if it is with his wife.

"Actually, when I first met Frank, I hated him!" Isabelle giggles. "Well, before I really met him, I knew of him. He was a few years older than me and had quite a reputation in our high school, but we didn't get together until years later. I'd left to work in Washington, but came back to town when my father got sick. Frank had started a construction company here and I ran into him in the supermarket one day."

"So was it love at second sight then?"

"Oh, no!" Isabelle says. "Frank was this big lunk of a guy, and I fancied myself quite the sophisticate."

As she's saying this I can picture it perfectly: young, muscular Frank Sands, looking a little like James Dean in *Rebel Without a Cause*—white undershirt with a pack of cigarettes rolled in the sleeve, denims, and work boots, meeting up with the delicate and pretty Isabelle. I envision her with a little scarf tied around her neck, looking chic and Frenchy, probably wearing capri pants and ballet flats. Their hands collide as they both reach for the same loaf of bread . . .

"Rammed his cart right into mine, right there in the frozen food section," she continues. "And it wasn't an accidental tap, Grace. He'd seen me staring into the freezer and purposely bumped into me."

"Ha! What'd you do?" I ask, pulling my knees up to my chest. "I probably would have chased him through the aisles until I had him cornered, then taken either the best *or* most embarrassing item out of his cart and held it hostage until he apologized."

Isabelle laughs. "That's what I should have done, but I just shrieked!" She shakes her head. "It was so *very* not cool of me, and it made getting back into the pose of cosmopolitan sophisticate downright impossible that afternoon."

"So what did *he* do?"

"Frank laughed at me and said, 'Well, normally I don't get that response from a girl until *after* I've asked her out!'"

I laugh again, thinking that sounds exactly like the Mr. Sands I know; a guy so cool and secure, he makes fun of himself with ease . . . not unlike Eric.

She smiles. "Though at first I was furious at this overly confident cart-bashing oaf, with that line, he charmed me. It made me realize that maybe, just maybe, some of my assumptions about this fellow had been wrong."

I nod. "I make an ass of myself by making assumptions about things all the time."

"Don't be so hard on yourself, Grace," replies Isabelle. "I'll bet your gut instincts are better than you're giving yourself credit for. But you're allowed to reassess and change your mind about things. Frank and I both learned that when I left him to go back to Washington."

My head tilts to the side. "Wait a minute," I break in, "you left him?"

"That's right. I stayed in town through my father's illness. But I had a life and a job I loved in DC. I'd been moving up the ranks at the Smithsonian Institution. American art and portraiture had been my specialty, and I'd been hoping to become head of the division, a rarity for a woman at that time. So I told Frank I was going and do you know what he said?"

"Was it something like, '*The hell you are!*'" I say in my best imitation of the Frank Sands grumble.

Isabelle shakes her head. "He said to me, and I quote, 'Well, I'll miss you.'"

"That was it?" This does not sound like the Mr. Sands I know. The Mr. Sands I know wouldn't have let the woman he loved get away. He always went after what he wanted—*stuck to his guns*, as he might say. "No, I don't believe it."

"Oh, yes."

"Were you surprised?"

"Surprised? I was so mad, I almost spit at him," Isabelle continues. "It's funny, sometimes you don't realize how much you want something until it's taken away. That's what happened when Frank said, 'I'll miss you.' But he didn't say, 'No! You can't go, Izzy, I won't let you.' He wasn't even saying 'please don't go.' Just, 'I'll miss you.'"

An interesting point: The person worth being with is the person who knows what you're worth and who fights to keep you. "But you two did wind up together—I mean, you're married now." Isabelle nods her head. "So what happened?"

"Do you know it took that man a year and a half to realize he'd let the best thing that ever happened to him slip through his fingers?" She laughs, fanning herself in mock modesty. "A year and a half! We'd kept in touch somewhat during that time, but it wasn't until I mentioned I'd gotten serious with a boy down in Washington that Frank Sands sprung into action. He hopped into his truck and didn't stop driving until he got to my front door. He said, 'Izzy, I felt more alive when we were together than I even knew possible. I want to feel that way again, and for the rest of my life.'"

I try to imagine how I'd respond to words like those. Try to picture the guy who would say something like that to me. "So, did you just jump into his arms at that point?"

"No," Isabelle responds with a devious smile. "I made him suffer. I told him he needed to convince me why I should choose him. Plus it was a little bit of revenge for him taking that long to come to his senses."

"I'm not sure I would have been able to pull that off. I probably would have thrown myself on him right then and there."

"Grace"—Isabelle shakes her head—"if you don't value yourself, no one else will either."

"My dad left my mom for another woman." This

comes out of my mouth before I even think about what I'm saying.

"Oh, Grace, I'm sorry, I know how hard something like that can be."

"Understatement," I mumble.

"And there isn't a thing in the world anyone else can say or do to make it better."

"Most people seem to make it worse." I pick at the threads in the knee of my jeans, wishing I hadn't brought this up.

Isabelle looks down at her hands, and seems to consider whether she should say more. "You're entitled to feel angry, you know. None of this was your doing and yet here you are in the middle of it."

I nod. "It's not fair."

"No, it's not. But I think when you're ready, letting the anger go will help a great deal."

"I don't think I'm there yet." Part of me doubts I'll ever be there.

"No rush." Isabelle shakes her head. "People act selfishly, Lord knows I have. Frank has too. No one—no one—is perfect."

Though this isn't exactly a newsflash, hearing the words now, it almost sounds like a revelation. "I'm afraid that doesn't change much even as we get older," she adds.

"So mentally we all just stay teenagers for the rest of our lives? Please do not tell me life is high school."

"More like middle school," Isabelle says with a laugh. "And you're wonderful, Grace, you really are. I thank you for coming here today, it means a lot."

"I don't think I've cheered you up too much."

"You've done better than that," she replies. "Because you and I, we haven't been pretending here, have we? Neither one of us is speaking to the other like she's a child. We've just been talking things through, the both of us understanding that life's messy and hard and constantly requires reexamination."

I nod and smile at Isabelle. I like her even though I don't want to. Liking her complicates things. Liking her means I'll probably wind up thinking about her . . . and worrying about her . . . which is the last thing I need. And because I know I shouldn't invest, because I know liking her will only make life more difficult, it makes her friendship that much more interesting to me.

♫ ♫ ♫

When I leave the cottage, determined to "embrace the suck" and deal, I head for Mr. Sands's room in the main building. His door is open, so I walk in. "Mr. Sands," I say, barreling forward and approaching his bed. "Have I got a story for you!" I want to keep things as breezy as possible this afternoon and get back to our usual banter.

"Grace," he says in a low, croaking voice. He doesn't

look good; his skin is dry and yellowy-gray, and a pungent smell comes from his mouth.

"Are you okay?"

I look at Mr. Sands lying there and take him in. I've never *really* looked at his body before because he's usually dressed in some sort of flannel shirt and chino pants. But today he's wearing a pajama top that's open enough at the neck that I can see the loose skin on his sternum that's threaded with blue veins. I watch his chest rise and fall, trying to get air. But instead of deep, rhythmic breaths in and out, its shallow, up and down movement makes it look like he's attempting to catch up to something, but he's falling helplessly behind. I wonder how Isabelle can stand to see him—the man who'd once rammed her supermarket cart, the man who'd pursued her to Washington— like *this*. I wonder if he asked her to "help" him too. Or if he asked me because people would suspect her involvement.

No one would ever think to question me . . . I'm just a kid with an after-school job in a nursing home.

"Do you want to play cards or checkers or something?" I finally say. "You know I might even let you win."

"No," he replies, "not just now."

"That's okay, I was just kidding. I wasn't going to let you win."

To my relief, this makes Mr. Sands laugh. "Oh, Grace," he softly slurs.

"I'm sorry," I reply, breaking eye contact and looking down at my shoes. "My stupid jokes probably aren't helping."

Slowly and with great effort, Mr. Sands says, "Your stupid jokes mean the world to me."

Whether it's from the tone or the sentiment, I'm suddenly overcome, and I try to smile as I feel hot tears sting the corners of my eyes. "Well then," I reply, "you're in luck, because stupid jokes, I've got a million of them."

"That's my girl," he says. "That's my Gracie."

And that's when "his girl," his "Gracie," has to look away, and my eyes fall on his nightstand. In my ear I can almost hear the words of his wife: "You're allowed to reassess and change your mind about things." Sometimes we make assumptions. Sometimes we make decisions. And sometimes they're wrong. Isabelle had said life requires reexamination, and I think she's right about that.

Chapter Nine

I figure it's worth a shot. Answers can come to you from strange places. And none would be stranger than my sister. "Hey, Lolly," I say when I get home and find her on the living room floor doing her homework in front of the TV. "How do you decide if you should do something if you're not sure if it's right or not?"

"Huh?" she says, without bothering to look at me.

"Okay," I reply, trying to figure out how to rephrase without giving away too much. "Have you ever been in a situation where somebody wants you to do something, but you're not sure that it's, like, moral?"

"Why?" she asks, her head suddenly jerking up. "What'd you hear?"

"Nothing, guilty conscience." I shake my head, taking a peanut M&M from the bag in my pocket and throwing it in her direction.

She snags it out of the air with her right hand and pops it into her mouth.

"So do you mean have I ever been in a position where I'm not sure if I should listen to my conscience or not?" she asks, then sits up crossing her legs, happy for the excuse to close her textbook. "Sure, of course I have."

"Really?" I take my coat off and plop down on the couch, slipping off my shoes and pulling my knees to my chin. "So how did you ultimately decide what to do or not do?"

But instead of answering that question, Lolly leans in close to me and grabs my pinky with hers. "Promise you won't tell Mom?"

I nod and we unlock our pinkies.

"Okay, well, Jake has been wanting me to have sex with him, right?"

"Uh—" I say, unprepared for the hard left turn my brain has to make to participate in *this* topic of conversation.

"But this is my virginity we're talking about, and I didn't want to give it up to just *anybody* because some guy's putting pressure on me. This is the kind of thing that has to be *my* decision. *I* have to be the one calling the shots on this, you know? That's the kind of thing that once it's gone, it's gone."

I nod and bite my bottom lip. I'm hearing Lolly's words but haven't gotten Mr. Sands out of my head yet.

"And I don't care what some of the girls at school say, you can't re-virginize if you don't sleep with anyone again for like a year."

"Re-virginize?" I ask, my eyes finally focusing on my sister.

"Yeah, like when you pick a cherry off a tree, another one grows back in a year. Same idea."

Though I'd tried to block out most of what we'd learned in sex ed, I definitely remembered the day our wrestling coach/health class teacher did the "breaking of the hymen" unit. Mr. Z. read the description directly from our text book: "It occurs when the male genitalia breaks the thin membrane that covers the opening of the vagina." Mr. Z. then looked up, smiled, and said, "And boys, best remember that old Pottery Barn slogan, 'You break it, you bought it.'" Most of the guys laughed uncomfortably, the girls' reactions seemed split between embarrassment and horror. I felt embarrassed, horrified, *and* nauseous.

"The girls at school think they can become born-again virgins? That's bird-brained. Why would they even say that?" I ask.

"Um, because they're sluts?" Lolly replies. "They're trying to pretend like they didn't do all that stuff. But once you make that decision it's obviously a done deal— no second chance to make a first 'impression.'" Lolly laughs.

"So you *didn't* have sex with Jake?" I feel a rush of relief, like a deep exhale.

"No." Lolly chews on the tip of her pen cap for a moment until the left side of her mouth curls into a smile. "Not yet."

Not *exactly* the answer I was hoping for, but close enough for now. And maybe this is Lolly's way of admitting she isn't as sure about Jake as she's been pretending. "You haven't had sex with him because you think, I don't know, he might be fooling around with other girls?"

"What?! *No*, that's not what I meant at all."

"Oh." I try to make it sound casual. "Then what? Something stopped you. What was it?"

"Well, I thought about it, but I want it to be special, and I realized that by making Jake wait a little while longer, he would respect me more." Lolly nods. "And it's working, because he understands what it means. He's not so in my face about it all the time anymore, so that tells me that he really gets it, you know?"

I nod. I did know. I knew he was "getting it" from another girl, and when the phone rings a moment later, I have a sick sense who's calling before I pick up.

"Lol?" Jake says when I answer.

"No, it's Grace," *you asshole.*

"Oh, hey," he replies casually. I wonder if he'll come up with some excuse about why he was kissing Natalie in the pharmacy the other day, some long-winded explanation of how he thought his tonsils were inflamed and Natalie said she'd be happy to examine them for him. "You know, I'd really like to see some of your art stuff next time I'm over at your house, okay?"

It is not okay.

"Hang on," I answer. "Lolly, it's Ja—" Before I even have the chance to finish his name, she springs to her feet and reaches for the receiver, wrestling it from my hand.

"Hey!" she says, sounding way too excited to hear from him. "Wait, I'm going to take this upstairs where I can get some privacy," Lolly says. After I hear her door close upstairs, the key turns in the lock of the front door. Mom pushes through and enters a moment later, a droopy-dog expression on her face.

"Hope you and your sister want hamburgers for dinner." She holds up two grease-stained white paper bags with the red You Say Potato . . . logo on the front.

"Yeah, that's fine," I respond. Whenever Mom brings food home from the restaurant, it usually means something unpleasant happened during her shift. I don't know whether they give it to her as compensation, or whether she takes it to compensate herself, and I don't ask. I do know, however, that if I'm still hanging around in another ten seconds, I'll be forced to hear all about it.

It's not so much that I mind listening to her stories. Everyone likes to have an audience—that's why most people have kids, isn't it? Sometimes her stories are even funny. (Like the time she told us about the busboy who wiped out while he was carrying the Caution! Slippery Floor sign across the dining room. Or when one of the managers introduced the four-appetizer combo he named the "Four Play." Trouble started when waitresses started asking customers if they wanted "some Four Play" before their entrée.) But most of the time when Mom talks about work, it's usually about how she "got into it" with someone else, and she wants me to tell her she was 100 percent right and the other person was totally wrong. The problem is, after she explains the situation and her response, I almost always think she was the one who screwed up.

"Can you believe when I told the chief operating officer that I needed more budgeted for advertising this quarter, he had the nerve to suggest my media plan was wrong?" she asked me last time. "So I told him, Jim, you think you can come up with a better plan, you can do it yourself!" She looked at me for confirmation but all I could do was bite my lip to stop myself from telling her she was probably lucky he didn't fire her then and there.

"Is your sister home?" Mom asks.

"On the phone."

She nods. "Hey, how was your day?"

I stop at the top of the landing and turn around to face her. The overhead light shines on the crown of Mom's head and illuminates her face. Most of her makeup has worn off, so the purple half-moons under her eyes are no longer concealed and her exhaustion is visible.

"My day? It was okay. It was fine."

"Good," she says. "Good," she repeats as she takes off her overcoat and walks toward the kitchen.

Dinner is eaten in silence as Mom, Lolly, and I seem equally content to marinate in our own thoughts. Lolly picks at her burger and the bottom half of the bun, which is all she allows herself to eat, and when she finishes her few bites of dinner, she pushes her chair out and scrapes her plate in the trash.

"I'm going out," she says.

"Okay," Mom replies, not bothering to ask where she's going or with whom.

I follow Lolly's lead, clean my plate, and run upstairs after her. "Where are you going?" I ask, finding her in the bathroom reapplying mascara.

"Out with Jake," she replies. "We'll probably watch a movie at his house." She looks at me out of the corner of her eye. "Or something," she adds with a mischievous grin.

I wonder what Mom would do if she knew what I did about Jake. And then I do the gut check Mr. Sands suggests: What's the right thing to do in this situation? By not telling Lolly that her boyfriend's a cheater, do I ultimately hurt her more than if I come clean about what I know?

The gut tells me to go for it: "You know, Lolly," I finally say, "I think you can do better than Jake."

She brings her right hand down and away from her face. "What?"

"I just mean you could date anyone you want, so—"

"Of course I *want* to be dating Jake. Do you have a problem with him or something?"

I shrug, then lean against the bathroom doorway. "I don't like him," I say quietly.

"He's never been anything but nice to you, so why is it that you don't like him all of a sudden?"

I open my mouth to respond, but the words don't come easily. "It's not all of a sudden. I just get a bad vibe from him."

"A bad vibe? What's that supposed to mean?" I can see she's getting mad now because a little blue lighting bolt vein crops up on the left side of her forehead. "Anyway, it doesn't really matter if you like him or not, because I'm the one dating him."

The gut says: *Only until you find out about him and Natalie.* "You're right," I reply instead. (Apparently my gut has an override switch.)

"Sometimes I don't understand you, Grace." Lolly shakes her head and returns to staring at her reflection.

I look at her in the mirror instead of looking at her directly, even though she's standing only two feet away from me. Somehow it's easier to talk to the image than the real person. "Don't you ever wonder about him and other girls, though? I mean, he's really flirty, don't you think?"

"So? All guys are like that. It doesn't mean anything."

"But what if it does?" I don't want to say it. I don't want to say it. And then I do: "What if I told you he really was cheating."

Lolly makes a laughing sound through her nose.

"I saw him."

"You *saw* him. You *saw* him cheating on me? Do you even know how stupid that sounds?"

"Lolly—"

"Enough, Grace." She puts both hands up in front of her, and the forehead vein flickers again. "I mean, I'm sorry you don't have a boyfriend. But I just think it's really sad that you want to wreck my relationship with Jake because no one wants to go out with you."

I can practically see myself as a cartoon character with steam shooting out of my ears and nostrils. "Wow. Wow, yup, that's exactly what I wanted to do. Just trying to bring you down because I'm a jealous loser." Skulking away from her, I head for my room.

The mirror over my bureau gives me a jolt. I now have a view of what I must look like to Lolly, and I don't like what I see either. There's a pot of lip gloss on the bureau and I swirl my middle finger in it, then smear it over my lips. I gather my hair to put it up in a ponytail, but the girl in the mirror now looks too little girly, so I decide to keep it loose, running my hands through my hair and mussing my bangs slightly. Not great, but a slight improvement. I grab my sweater and take a final glance back at myself in the mirror before walking out of the room.

I run downstairs, open the front door, and hop on my bike. Riding in the direction of Eric's house, it's like I'm on auto-pilot. Whatever it was that initially stopped me from accepting his invitation to the dance—pride?— well, I'm just going to let that go and tell him we'll go together. I dial Eric's number as I approach his house.

111

"Grace," Eric says when he picks up. "What's up?"

"Guess where I am?"

"You're calling me from the trunk of a vehicle speeding toward the border. Your captors mistakenly thought you'd be an excellent candidate to sell into white slavery."

"I'm on your block."

"Or you're on my block."

"I like your version better," I say. "Everything except the part about me being locked in a trunk and sold into slavery."

"Mine is slightly more cinematographic than yours, this is true," Eric replies. "But I do have a director's eye."

"And a psycho's mind."

"You know a guy can only hear that so many times a day without starting to get paranoid." He laughs. "So you want to come over? Or are you just planning to hide in my bushes the whole night—speaking of psychos."

"Well, I didn't want to just drop by unannounced in case you were doing something . . . I don't know, weird."

"Uh-huh, be careful with the pervert talk, you might start giving me ideas, Manning. Hmm, I wonder how much someone like you would fetch if I tried selling you into white slavery?"

When I get to the Wards' door, Eric greets me with, "Heads up!" tossing a Granny Smith apple at me.

"Hey," I yelp, quick enough to get my hand up, but not

fast enough to catch the apple, which ends up bouncing against my palm and dropping to the ground.

"Reflexes, Grace," Eric says with a smile and a shake of the head. "We're going to have to work on those reflexes."

"I don't think your mom would be too happy to learn you're greeting visitors by pelting them with fruit."

"Point, Manning." Eric grimaces. "Okay, you've won this round, but I'll get you next time, my pretty." He proceeds to twist his imaginary mustache at both ends. "Come on, it's good you're here, you need to quiz me for our American History test."

"We're having a test in American History?"

"Uh, yeah? This is the test on the Vietnam conflict, recall?"

"Ah," I say as we head upstairs to his room, "the war not deemed a war because we lost."

"And why else was it a 'conflict' instead of a war?" Eric presses in a professorial tone.

"Because there were no clear combat zones; there was no front. Territory was taken, lost, and taken back again."

"And why else?" Eric asks as he sits down at his desk and I plop down on his bed.

"Because Congress never officially declared it a war."

"Very good. And, for the bonus round"—he holds up his index finger—"*why else?*"

"Because we had no plan," I say, not realizing I'd absorbed so much of this stuff. "No exit strategy. Even when it was clear there was no way to win—that no good could come from sticking around and fighting more, we just kept slogging on and on."

Eric nods. "Pointless suffering."

We study for the next forty-five minutes straight, going over his class notes and making up quiz questions from the textbook. When I get the fifth of five lightning round questions correct, I shrug at Eric like it's no big deal. "Look, I just want to say you don't have to be intimidated by my brilliance, because I promise I will never wield it against you."

"Z'at right?" he snorts, crumpling up a piece of paper and throwing it at me. This time my reflexes are primed and I catch it.

"Ah-ha!" I yell. "The student has become the teacher." I stand up and take a step closer to Eric so that when I throw the paper ball back at him, it bounces right off his shoulder.

"Not so fast, grasshopper!" he yells back, scooping the ball up from the ground. His arm cocks into pitching position and I take a fast step backward to get as far away from him as I can. Unfortunately I get tangled up in a stray sneaker in the middle of the floor and shriek as I find myself falling back onto his bed.

"Ha!" Eric laughs, hurling the paper missile at me, the momentum carrying him a foot forward and directly into the path of that sneaker. "Ahh!" he yells as he pitches forward and falls on top of me.

Our mutual clumsiness causes us both to start laughing so hard we nearly knock heads as Eric unsuccessfully tries to raise himself up off me. With one hand pushing against the bed, and the other pushing on my right thigh, he hoists himself up. But the pressure he puts on my leg tickles, and I collapse backward in another fit of giggles, my hands flopping on either side of my head.

"You!" I say between laughs and gasps for air.

"Oh, yeah?" Eric replies, his hands grabbing mine, his body hovering above me.

Eric's face is now only inches from my own and when I look into his light blue eyes, I'm not entirely sure what I'm expecting. But he returns my stare, and I see he's really looking at me. My lips part and suddenly I'm not laughing anymore, just exhaling. I move my chin up and bring my lips closer to Eric's mouth. He keeps his eyes open as he brings his lips to meet mine, and as soon as they touch, I close my eyes. His lips are soft and warm and have a faint taste of the Starbucks iced coffee drink that's sitting next to his keyboard.

I've never had someone else's tongue in my mouth before, and I'm glad in another minute I'll never have to say that again. I can feel Eric's mouth opening and the hot air circling between us. Our hands remain clenched by my head, and Eric is using his arms and his knees to keep himself propped up in a position that can't be comfortable for him. Still, I'm not sure what to encourage him to do. Would he even want me to say anything at this moment? Do people do that? As I feel Eric's tongue on my teeth, I realize I'm supposed to open my mouth wider and when I do, our tongues touch. It feels a lot less bizarre than how I'd been imagining it all these years.

So it's this? I think.

This is the thought that takes me out of the moment and back into my own head. This is one of those events I've been thinking about my whole life. One of those things that you always wonder how it's going to feel but you just can't know—not even if someone describes it really well—until you do it yourself. Like what it feels like to be the one driving a car, or like what it feels like to skydive or go under anesthesia. My eyes pop open and I try to bring my concentration back to Eric.

"Grace," he says.

"Am I doing something wrong?"

Eric shakes his head.

"Should we stop?" I ask.

The question has the force of an answer and he pulls back. "Well," he says after he scrutinizes my face for another minute. "Do you want to?"

I nod quickly, not wanting to say anything for fear of hurting his feelings, but not wanting to go any further now. I know I need to explain myself in some way. But all I can manage is, "What if your mother comes in?"

"Yeah," he replies, both of us knowing this would never happen. Neither one of us says anything for a minute—a silence so awkward, it's unbearable.

"Maybe I should go. My mom's probably going to be expecting me home soon anyway," I say lamely.

"Okay." He rolls over on the bed and doesn't look at me.

"I . . ." I re-tuck my shirt and scramble off the bed. "So I'll see you later." I reach for the doorknob and close it softly behind me as I leave.

As I run down the stairs and out Eric's front door, the sentence *What did I do?* keeps running through my head. But eventually that makes way for another one: *What is Eric going to think of me?* And eventually that's pushed out by yet another thought: *Will this change everything?*

Chapter Ten

In my dictionary, the first definition of the word *refuge* is "a place or state of safety," and though I get it, I don't think it's quite right. The first time I'd heard the word was when we learned about the "protected territory for animals and wild life" in Earth Science class in middle school. But then in World History, we learned about "refugees," who are people who flee to a foreign country to escape danger. In our philosophy unit in Civics, we learned that the first step in becoming a Buddhist is to "take refuge," which means to "look into oneself."

My problem with the dictionary's definition isn't that it doesn't include these differences because, in a way, "a place or state of safety" does get to the basic sense of all of these ideas. *My problem* is that I think the dictionary writers are making too big an assumption. They're saying safety can be assured in a designated location, and I'm not so sure it can. I mean, are you *ever* entirely safe? Are you safe in a school yard? Crossing the street? In the bathtub? You can slip and fall anywhere. You can also slip up, fall ill, or be persecuted, taunted, or haunted in any spot. And it's especially difficult to find a place of "refuge" when the things that are tormenting you—the things you'd most like to run from—are the thoughts that keep running through your own head.

I barely sleep at all that night, freaked out by what happened between Eric and me and still jangled by thoughts of Mr. Sands, which keep crashing through my head. When I get out of bed the next morning, I just feel the need to flee. But since I can't find refuge, I decide to settle for a "sanctuary" instead. The chapel at Hanover House is located near the cafeteria, and it seems as good a place as any to hide for a while. Forget school, I just need time to think. About everything. I don't bother showering when I wake up, I just layer my green "COLLEGE" T-shirt over my softest long-sleeve shirt and slip into a pair of jeans that were washed relatively recently (I think). I grab my book bag, hop on Big Blue, and start pedaling so quickly, a cramp stabs my gut. I knead the area with my fingers instead of slowing my pace. When I get to the main building of Hanover House, I keep my head down as I walk, not wanting to make eye contact with anyone, hoping no one will notice that a school kid isn't in school this morning. I safely make it to the chapel. But the sound of the door whooshing open makes the man sitting alone in the third row turn around.

"Oh, sorry," I say, "I didn't know anyone was going to be here now. I'll go."

"You don't need to leave," he replies, shaking his

head. "This place is supposed to be here for everyone, right?"

"I guess." I shrug.

The man gives a half smile. "I'm pretty sure I'm right."

"Okay." I nod, sliding into one of the back pews.

The man turns around and lays his arms on top of the pew in front of him, resting his head on top of them. I stare at the way his shoulders connect with his back and think he looks like he's preparing for a swim race. From the way he's concentrating, I'd bet he was the guy who swam butterfly when he was in school. But he only stays still for another minute, then turns back around to see if I'm still here.

I try to look away as quickly as I can, but he catches me staring. "My mother," he says, as if he's the one who owes the explanation, "she's not doing very well."

"That's too bad, I'm sorry," I reply. I don't know if I'm supposed to say anything more or just let him get back to doing whatever he was doing, but he doesn't turn away.

"Is a grandparent of yours here?" he asks.

I consider the advantages of lying: I wouldn't have to explain why I'm not in school—people with dying relatives get a pass on cutting. And it's not like he'd doubt me; the age thing works out about right. I mean, this guy even sort of looks like my dad. "No," I say, "I work here."

He smiles. "You work here?"

"I'm a candy striper."

"Oh." He nods, looking like he either doesn't quite get it or doesn't quite buy it.

"Yeah, I get credit at my high school for working here," I lie, nodding vigorously, so he'll believe me. That's when the toreador text ring tone goes off. "Oh, sorry," I say, quickly reaching around to find my phone in my bag.

CNT BLVE U CUT TST! WHR RU?

Eric.

The Vietnam test.

Shit.

My thumbs start moving before I'm even sure what I'm going to say. DEATHLY ILL, I type, then hit SEND, guiltily looking back up at the man sitting in the front of the chapel. "Sorry about that," I say again.

"Important message?" he asks.

"Uh, I just had to let someone know where I—"

Duh-duh-duhn-nuh-nuh-duh-dun-duhn-nuh-nuh-nuh the phone chimes.

"Sounds like someone's pretty interested in your answer," the guy says with a smile. I glance down at Eric's response and I'm not sure "interested" is the word I would choose; "pissed" is more like it.

Y RU LYNG 2 ME?

I snap the phone shut. This is not something I feel like I can explain on the keypad of my cell phone.

"Yeah, I guess," I say.

"So what does a candy striper here do?" the man asks.

"I'm still sort of trying to figure that out. But, uh, we're basically supposed to befriend the residents, and make things more comfortable for them, water their plants, give them magazines . . ." *Consider the idea of helping them end their suffering.*

"Well, I'm sure they appreciate that. I know I would. I'm always impressed by people who selflessly try to help others like you're doing. Strikes me as very"—the man puts his arms out—"Christian."

I bite down on the inside of my lip. "I don't think handing out celebrity magazines really qualifies as Christian."

"The Lord works in mysterious ways."

"Can I ask you a question?" I say suddenly.

"Oh." He blinks. "Sure."

"I mean, if this is too personal, just tell me to shut up or whatever."

He laughs a little. "Now you've got my attention."

"Do you think this works?" I motion to the pews, the altar. When he doesn't answer right away, I figure I need to be more specific. "The praying. I mean, do you really think anyone's listening?"

"Yes," he says, nodding his head. "But I suppose that's going to be the answer you get from most people you'd find in a church."

"Dumb question, I know."

"No, no, I didn't mean that. I just meant that that's probably just the knee-jerk reaction you'd get from most people. People don't really like to think about it because it's more reassuring to them to have a definite answer. Having an answer is a comfort. It's when you start asking questions and those questions pull threads in the larger fabric, you're forced to wonder what you're left with. And for people of any age, it's scary to think the fabric of the universe—or the universe as you've always believed it existed—can just unwind, you know?"

"Yep." I start thinking of all the "absolutes" that used to exist for me. I realize my head is tilting to the side as I try to figure out if he just told me he believed in prayer because it's easier to believe that or because he really *really* believes it does work. "So you think someone hears us or is listening when we pray?"

He smiles and I can see both the top and bottom rows of his teeth. "I've had moments of doubt. Of course I have. I don't know how anyone can live in this world where, let's face it, injustice takes place all the time, and *not* wonder if anyone's paying attention." He shrugs. "But what I keep coming back to is the fact that life is so fragile, someone has to be looking out for us. At least in the most basic way. So for me, prayer is not just the asking of a favor—like 'please God, let my mother be okay'—but as more of a thank you. A thank you for every minute I've had with her. I'm sure that kind of sounds corny, but it does help me appreciate the good things in my life. So when I say yeah, prayer works, it's because I think that if all I'm doing here is expressing gratitude for her life, that's okay. That's important."

This certainly isn't the answer I'm expecting. But it is kind of interesting.

"Do you?" he asks.

"Do I what?"

"Believe?" the man says.

My first instinct is to say yes. Because he's right, it'd be the easiest answer. "I don't really know anymore," I say instead. "I want to."

"You do?"

"Well yeah."

"Why?" he asks.

Why? Why do I *want* to believe? Now that was a question I'd never even thought of before. Why do I want to believe? "I dunno. Part of it's probably that I like to think someone is listening when I do check in or ask a favor."

"Well, what is it that you want? What are you asking for?" He puts his hands on his thighs and his elbows stick out as he leans forward on his bench back toward me.

There are a million answers to this question: I want everything to be okay. I want Mr. Sands to be healthy. I want things to be normal with Eric. I don't want to fail biology. I want to be prettier. I want to be able to speed read. I want world peace. I never want to get a zit again. I want to be able to eat anything I want and not gain weight. I want to be talented at something. I want to know Isabelle will be okay if I help Mr. Sands. I want to smell nice all the time. I want my dad to apologize for leaving. And then I want him to come back and stay. I want to live happily ever after. And I don't want to have to think about these things.

"Just the normal stuff, I guess."

"You're not cutting school to hang out in the chapel of an old-age home on a Friday because you want the normal stuff," he says. I shift uncomfortably on the horrible wooden bench. The man shakes his head. "Don't worry, I'm not going to alert the authorities and I don't mean to pry. I just wish I could help you."

It's been a long time since I've heard anyone say that to me. "Thanks," I say, looking down, feeling tears start.

"Is there anyone you can talk to?" he asks. And when I look back up at him, then roll my eyes upward, he smiles. "Oh, right," he replies.

"I should probably . . ." I stand to leave, just letting the thought trail.

"Well, I'll include you in my prayers. I'll make it pretty general." He clasps his hands together. "Just one of those 'thank you for giving this young woman the faith she needs to get her through.'"

"How do you know I have it?"

"Because *I* have faith," he replies.

I exit the chapel and walk toward Mr. Sands's room, knowing that he's someone I can talk to. He's given me sanctuary before too, and he'll understand why I'm cutting school. But I stop short in the hallway when I see Isabelle inside with another woman. The younger woman is dressed in a navy pantsuit with a pretty silk blouse underneath, and looks to be about my mom's age. I've never seen her before, but from the way she's leaning over Mr. Sands, I assume she's one of their two daughters. I'd like to meet her, but there'd be too much explaining if I went in now. So I move away from the door and for the next few hours I just move from one low-traffic area of Hanover House to another, hoping I won't arouse suspicion.

I haven't let myself look at my watch for a while now, figuring that I'd only be disappointed to see how slowly time was moving. But when I finally take a peek, I'm pleasantly surprised to see that it's past 2:17 p.m., and the school day is officially over. I can finally go home and once again be miserable in the privacy of my own bedroom. As I walk down the hall on my way to one of the side exits, though, I catch a glimpse of a pretty blond ponytail and for a moment I think it's Natalie Talbot. I take a step back and look again: It *is* Natalie Talbot.

"Grace?" Natalie yells, stopping me in my tracks. "Hey, I thought that was you." She walks toward me. "One of your grandparents is here too?"

Since I'm not wearing my candy striper apron, I probably look like any other normal visitor at Hanover House—nervous, uncomfortable, and anxious to leave.

"Actually I work here."

"Really?" Natalie's nose wrinkles. "Does that mean you have to, like, change the bedpans and stuff?"

"My job's more like handing out copies of *Us Weekly* and bringing mail to the residents."

"Ah, so you get to see all the new magazines all the time?"

"Usually they're a little old." I shrug. "I mean, it's not like anyone here really cares when they learn about some star's new baby or who's hooking up with who, just as long as they get a general idea so they can talk to their grandkids about it."

"That kind of sounds like fun." Natalie smiles, almost making me think she means it. "Hey, come into my grandfather's room!"

Before I say "Gotta run!" she's already slipped inside, and for some reason I find myself following right behind her.

It's not a private room like the one Mr. Sands has; instead there are two beds with patients inside, separated by a "privacy" curtain that looks like it runs on a zipper attached to the ceiling. The person in the half of the room near the door clearly gets shafted on the privacy part, because all visitors have to tromp through his space first. But I guess a lot of people here aren't really in the position to complain, or notice really. Since I don't see Natalie when I walk in, I assume her grandfather is in the second slot on the other side of the thin curtain, and have to smile at the unhappy-looking guy in bed #1 as I pass by.

"He's been out of it for a week," Natalie says. "Think he knows we're here?" She passes her hand over his face like a magician doing a spell.

"Yes," I respond immediately.

"Do they pay you to say that?" she laughs. "Like I always wondered if that wasn't just something they tell you to make you feel guilty for not visiting people here more often."

"No, I don't think there's any conspiracy to make people feel guilty. I think feeling guilty just comes naturally around this place."

Natalie laughs. "Oh, wait, do you need to get back to work or something? I don't want to keep you if you're going to get in trouble. But it's nice to have company in here."

"Thanks," I say, and then, before I can stop myself, add, "Hey, can I ask you something?"

"Sure," she says, pointing me to the chairs.

"Why were you kissing Jake the other day?" I don't know why I need to know the answer to this right now, but I do. Maybe it's just that if anyone would seem to have all the answers, it'd be a girl like Natalie.

"What?" She looks down. "What are you talking about? I wasn't kissing Jake."

"Natalie, I saw you," I say, cocking my head to the side in the *why are you lying to me?* position, "at the Fulton Pharmacy?"

"Yeah, I know," she replies, examining the hem on her skirt, "we had that whole conversation about the green Blow Pops. And we were in total agreement that sour apple is the best flavor." She glances back up at me to see if I'll let it go.

But if I've waded this deeply into awkward territory, why back away now? "No," I respond, "I mean I saw you two before that. In the reflection of the shoplifter mirror."

"Oh, you mean when we were in the beverage section?" she asks, as if she hasn't just been caught in a lie, but rather that this must just be another question. "Yeah, well, see, Rich and I—Rich is my boyfriend, or *was* anyway—so we've been fighting a lot lately. He'd been acting like a total dick since he got back from his college recruitment visits. Like he's suddenly way too cool for school now that some soccer coach at UVA expressed interest, you know?"

I have no idea.

"So anyway," she continues, twisting her hair into a low ponytail by her right shoulder, "I know it probably wasn't the best way of handling it, but I knew it would make Rich jealous if I hooked up with Jake. Especially with Jake," Natalie laughs, "because he and Rich used to be friends. But something happened between them and of course they won't talk to each other about it because they're *boys*, so they just kind of let it fester."

"Uh-huh." I nod.

"Anyway, I know your sister and Jake had been going out, so how's she taking the breakup?"

"Lolly and Jake haven't broken up," I say with a shake of the head.

"No, they did," replies Natalie, no trace of doubt in her voice. "Maybe she just hasn't said anything 'cause Jake told me things had gotten really weird between them and she was acting kind of—" She pauses and bites her lip.

"Kind of what?"

"Well, I don't really want to say anything bad because she's your sister."

"That's *exactly* why you have to tell me," I say.

Natalie nods, then looks me directly in the eye. "Okay, well, she started acting kind of stalker-y. Like, psycho, you know?"

Natalie's large green eyes look so open and honest, there seems no reason to doubt her, which is exactly why I need to stand up for Lolly. If Natalie had said she'd just been acting "bitchy," it wouldn't seem like such a big deal. The word *bitch* is so overused, it's practically meaningless. But being called a psycho is different because it's impossible to defend against. If you try proving you're not crazy, you usually just wind up doing something stupid. Then the response is: "See?

Told you she was a nut job." So as I watch Natalie blink her curled golden eyelashes, I know I can't let her judgment sit on my sister.

"I think *Jake's* the one who's acting crazy. He's telling her one thing and you another."

"Well." Natalie shakes her head, certain that the version she has is right. "I don't know what he said to Lolly, but I'd feel terrible if she thought they were still dating, because Jake said he only wanted to go out with me." Natalie takes my hand between hers. "Now I feel like I'm responsible for breaking them up, and I swear I never meant to do that."

That she actually looks upset surprises me. "Natalie, *you* didn't break them up. It was Jake. No one was exactly holding a gun to his head and forcing him to kiss you. He did that all on his own. *He's* the one who cheated." I don't say this to make her feel better. I say it because I really don't believe it was her fault. She might have been a temptation. But cheaters act with their own free will, a subject I spent a long time thinking about when my dad left us.

"Really? Okay, thanks," she replies, giving me a hug as if I've just pardoned her for her sins. "God, now that I know he did that to Lolly, I don't even want anything to do with him anymore."

"It's not like you have to," I say.

"Well . . ." Natalie quickly glances back to her grandfather. "I already agreed to go to the dance with Jake, so I'm kind of stuck with him through that weekend."

"So?" I shrug, following her eye line from her grandfather back out the window. "Tell him you changed your mind. Big deal if he gets upset or left alone. He deserves it."

"I know you're right, but—" Natalie puts her index finger between her front teeth and bites down on it. "I also told Rich I was going with Jake, and you just should have seen the look on his face. It was classic."

"Just find someone else to go with." I put my hands out to show her what a no-brainer this one is.

"Right," Natalie laughs, "like it would be that easy."

"For you it would be." And she laughs again like she doesn't believe me. "Are you kidding?" I say, "I, personally, know several guys who'd kill to go with you."

She puts her hands on her hips. "Like who?"

"Like who? Like everyone. Like my friend Eric, for instance. I mean, he even told me he thinks you're totally hot. But whatever, that's beside the point. You should follow your gut on this, and you shouldn't worry about what those boys will think. It's your decision and your conscience, you know?"

"I guess. I mean, I'll think about it." Natalie considers this for a moment, then looks down at her watch. "Okay, well anyway, I've probably stayed here long enough. Karma points earned, check please! Right?" She tosses her hair, then walks back over to her grandfather and awkwardly reaches over the bed's metal railing to kiss him on the forehead. "Bye, Pop-pop. Love you. I'll see ya, Grace." Natalie smiles, giving me a slight nod of the head before she walks out of the room just ahead of me.

"Nothing's ever easy, is it?" I ask under my breath as I follow her out. Unsurprisingly, Natalie's grandfather doesn't respond. "Yeah, that was my guess too."

Chapter Eleven

I haven't eaten all day, and I'm so hungry by the time I get home, the only thing I can think about is the can of Pringles I plan to dive into when I get inside. The salty tang should do a nice job of stopping the pain echoing in my stomach and head. But when I walk into the house, I find Lolly sprawled out on the couch, looking disheveled, like she hasn't showered or bothered combing her hair. Jake must have done it. He must have told her about Natalie and broken her heart.

"Hey," I say. I lean against the side of the couch and grab her foot. "I'm sorry about you and Jake." I shake her foot back and forth a little in what I hope seems like a gesture of understanding; considering what went on with Eric, if there's one thing I get right now, it's the need to have people be there for each other when everything feels like it's gone to hell.

"What are you talking about?" Lolly replies.

"Your breakup?"

"We didn't break up," she says emphatically.

"You didn't?"

"Nooooo," she says, her tone now implying that she's speaking to a vegetable. "Why would you even ask that?"

Getting out of here as quickly as I can seems to be my only move now, so I head for the kitchen. "Oh, uh, I don't know," I say over my shoulder, wishing I could hit REWIND/DELETE.

"Who told you we broke up?" Lolly asks, bolting upright from the couch.

"I can't exactly remember."

"Well, we didn't. We *definitely didn't* break up," Lolly says, punctuating each word in the sentence.

"Okay, I believe you. Sorry."

But this doesn't satisfy her. "I mean, if we'd broken up, would Jake have given me *this* this morning?" She walks over to me and points to an ugly reddish-purple hickey on her neck, which looks more like a wound than a sign of devotion.

"You're right, Lolly," I reply, feeling the heat rising to my cheeks. "If a hickey doesn't say 'I'll love you forever,' it's hard to know what does."

"Who told you we broke up?"

"It doesn't matter. If you say you haven't broken up, you should know, right?" I walk into the kitchen, but Lolly follows me.

"Tell me! Or are you just bullshitting again, Grace?"

This is not the time to be pushing me. "You want to know who it was? Do you *really* want to know who told me?" I ask, looking her directly in the eye. We're both priming for a fight, as if hurting the other will somehow make each of us feel better.

"Yeah," she says, "Grace, tell me. Where'd you get your juicy gossip?"

"Natalie Talbot." I cross my arms in front of me and stare at my sister to see how she'll react.

She laughs.

"Oh-kay!" replies Lolly. "Right, sure she did, because you and Natalie are such great friends." Then she shakes her head. "Just because you have some sort of problem with Jake, that's no reason to start making things up."

"Think what you want," I say. My cheeks are burning now. "But according to Natalie, you and Jake are done. And she would probably know since she's the one he dumped you for."

"You know what?" Lolly's voice is much calmer than I would have expected. "I think that's so funny, I'm going to call Jake right now and tell him what you said."

"Go ahead." I shrug. "But I wouldn't if I were you."

"Well, then it's good for us both that you're not." She takes the kitchen phone out of its cradle and punches in Jake's number.

"You'll regret it," I say, realizing she's serious about calling him. Then, "Don't."

"Now you're scared you're going to get called on your shit."

I look at my sister and suddenly that righteous feeling I'd had—the feeling of watching someone get a well-earned slap—starts fading into a much less cool sensation of knowing she's about to get hurt.

"Hey," Lolly says into the phone. "Nothing . . . Well, actually, my little sister and I were having a chat here and you are never going to believe what she just came up with. Grace just told me she heard that we'd broken up."

"Lolly, don't do this." I lunge for the phone.

"Get away from me," she yells, pulling it back to her ear. "So, Jake, do you want to tell Grace yourself how ignorant she is? I mean, do you know she even said that Natalie Talbot told her that we'd broken up?" Lolly cocks her head to the side and narrows her eyes at me as she awaits his response. But even though I can't hear what he's saying on the other end, it's pretty clear that it's not the firm denial my sister was looking for. "What?" she says. "What do you mean?" There's another pause as I see the information seeping into Lolly's body. "I don't believe this," she finally bleats, her voice no longer full of bravado, now sounding smaller, as if she's deflating. "Why would you . . . You know what? Whatever. I just can't believe you'd do something this shitty. I was even going to . . . You're such an asshole!"

Lolly jabs at the END button on the phone and throws it on the kitchen counter.

"Lolly, I'm sorry," I say, looking down.

"Oh, I'll bet you are," she hisses. "You loved that, didn't you? You loved telling me he cheated on me. You probably couldn't wait to do it." Her voice catches in the beginning of a sob and she storms out of the kitchen, then loudly runs up the stairs.

I wait to hear her door slam—which it does a few seconds later—then I open the cabinet next to the refrigerator. But instead of pulling out the potato chips, my eyes land on a jug of maple syrup.

Pancakes.

That's what I really want. So I take out two eggs, a stick of butter, and a carton of milk. I grab the flour, sugar, salt, vanilla, and baking powder from the pantry and start beating the ingredients together with Mom's old hand mixer. As I spin the mixer around the bowl, watching the chunks of butter break and fold into the batter, I'm mesmerized by the pattern the beaters spin into it. I keep moving the mixer around and around the bowl until the thick batter looks almost silky. My hand starts to ache from the movement and weight of the mixer, but the pain, so simple and easy to locate, is almost a relief. You're supposed to leave a few lumps so the batter doesn't spread too thin when you pour it. Thin is *not* an attractive pancake trait. So when I've beaten away all but the last few lumps and imperfections, I detach the mixer blades and lick them clean.

The round griddle, which I find packed away in a high cabinet above the oven, hasn't been used in a long time and it takes me a while to free it from under all the other random and rarely used kitchen crap stored up there.

My father had given it to my mother as a Mother's Day present. Even at age eleven I knew Mom wasn't going to be pleased by the gift. Mom didn't talk to him for the rest of the day. When she finally spoke to him the next morning at breakfast—for which Dad made pancakes— I remember hearing the word *selfish* thrown around a lot. I also remember Dad yelling back that everything he did, he did for the family. When Mom snorted, he said her problem was that she'd never had faith in him. He said a man couldn't fully exist without others believing in him, and that it was killing him. Mom said if he needed her to believe in him so badly, he had to provide more than hokey promises for the future.

The first Sunday after Dad left—the first Sunday I missed church and our pancake brunch—I spent the day wondering if the reason Dad was now with Nancy Falton was because she believed in him more than Mom did, and whether that made his decision okay. It's like that question "If I am not for myself, who will be for me? But if I am only for myself, who am I?"

I wipe off the griddle, then grease it before putting it on the stove and turning on the heat. As I drop generous dollops of batter on the griddle, I stay focused on the symmetry of the circles I create, which expand before they shrink again on the hot surface. I smile when I see the air bubbles pop to the surface—I always do—and today I think they make it look like some spirit inside the molten batter is trying to escape. I flip each pancake when it becomes firm, and they slide off the spatula with ease, leaving no chunks of batter behind. Once they've turned the perfect shade of golden brown, I take my stack of eight over to the kitchen table. I don't know how long the jug of Aunt Jemima syrup has been sitting in the cabinet, but I don't really care, and I squirt what remains all over the huge mound of pancakes.

I take the first bite and close my eyes to block out any other sight, sound, thought, or feeling. I do this with every bite thereafter, chewing as slowly and deliberately as I can. I tear through pancake after pancake, kneading each bite against the roof of my mouth with my tongue. I run my index and middle fingers through the stream of syrup pooled on the sides of the plate, then lick them clean.

But something's off.

Eating pancakes alone isn't the same; it almost feels like I'm missing some of my taste buds. For the girl who used to guard her plate so that no one would reach a fork over to steal a bite, the need to share this experience feels strange. I pick up the phone and dial Dad's number.

"Hullo?" he says. But the fact that his voice still sounds exactly the same when so much else has changed isn't a comfort, it somehow seems unfair. He should be affected too.

I can't do it.

It's too much.

I hang up and set the phone down on the kitchen table, biting my lip as I push my plate away.

༄ ༄ ༄

The last communication I had with Eric was our series of text messages on Friday when he accused me of lying to him about being sick. The last time we saw each other, my face and lips were pressed against his and then I ran out of his bedroom. So when he called over the weekend, I screened and didn't return the call because I didn't know what to say and it was just another thing I couldn't handle. When I see him at school this morning I don't have any clearer idea of what to say to him, so playing it cool—or as cool as I'm capable—feels like my only move.

"Hey," I say, approaching Eric at his locker. "What's up?"

"Hi." Eric continues unloading his book bag, and I keep standing there like an idiot. *Hi,* that's all I get.

"So how was the Vietnam test?"

He slams the top half of his locker shut with his palm. "Well, you would know if you'd called me back."

"I—I wanted to," I reply, looking down and away, "but my mom took away my 'weekend phone privileges' again." The lie comes out easily enough.

Eric stops, seeming to consider this. "Because she caught you cutting?"

"No," I say, wanting the reason to be even more

extreme. "See, I told Lolly that her relationship with Jake was over, and she went ballistic. *Then* Mom started hassling me and I was just so done with the whole thing, I told her that that was exactly the type of behavior that caused Dad to leave." The lie keeps rolling.

"You said that to your mom?" he asks, squinting. It's hard to read what Eric makes of this, so I just shrug. "Harsh."

"Yeah, I know," I reply, "I just kind of lost my head."

Eric nods, then turns back and closes the bottom half of the locker. I start to get a vague sense of relief that this explanation could have done the trick until he turns on his heel and faces me. "Grace, look." Eric's head dips forward. "The reason I wanted to talk to you was because I'm trying to figure out what's going on with us. You know chatting about feelings or whatever isn't exactly my thing, but aren't we supposed to talk about what went on the other night?"

In front of me is the guy I've been friends with since fourth grade, and he's staring at me so closely right now, it feels like I'm standing naked in the school hallway. What is he seeing? What is he thinking? On the one hand I want to know, but on the other, what if, in a chat like that you discover the other person—the one person you look forward to seeing more than anyone else—doesn't like you as much as you like him? *Would I really be better off or happier knowing that?*

"Well, it doesn't have to be a big deal," I say, now

turning my attention to my shoes. "We *could* just agree not to talk about what happened that night and then we wouldn't have to worry about it, right?"

Eric opens his mouth but doesn't say anything for a moment. "We could, but I mean—"

"Yeah, you know, this way there won't be any weirdness and we can just go back to the way things have always been, right?" I let my eyes tag Eric's, then I give him a playful punch on the shoulder.

"You're sure?" he says, making it sound like he just bit into something that tastes a little funky.

"Absolutely," I reply, absolutely sure of nothing.

"Okay." He nods. "I guess I'll see you at lunch then."

♪♫ ♪♫ ♪♫

Lunch.

Terrifying.

I sit down at an empty table and half expect Eric not to show up. The thought of again eating alone—especially in the middle of a crowded cafeteria—is almost sickening. But he does come, and when Eric takes the seat next to me, he nods, making me feel like an awful friend for doubting him. When I see Natalie and Jake talking at the front of the lunchroom, I can't resist bringing us back to a conversation that I know will spark Eric's interest.

"What do you think they're saying?" I ask him, nudging my head in Natalie's direction.

"Well," Eric replies, "if I'm Natalie, I'm looking at Jake and wondering what it ever was that I saw in him. And I'm probably saying something like, 'Jake, you jerk, why is it that you're not buying my lunch for me, carrying me piggyback to our lunch table, and insisting I cross puddles by stepping on your head.'"

"I can see that," I reply, watching as Jake begins gesticulating somewhat more aggressively. "And I'll bet now he's saying, 'But Natalie, my friends will think I'm whipped if I throw rose petals on the ground wherever you walk—I mean, I want to—but I have a reputation to uphold.'"

Eric laughs and continues in his Natalie voice, "Oh, Jake, that's so funny—you don't have a reputation. And let's be real, you couldn't be more whipped! I mean look at me, tee hee!"

"But Natalie," I say, staring at Jake, who is now rather wildly moving his hands in a chopping motion, "you know I'd do the Tomahawk Chop for you as many times as you asked me to. But I'm a dude, and we dudes need some sugar."

Eric rolls his eyes and breaks character. "We dudes need some sugar?" he repeats.

"Look, just because I live in a house of crazy women does not mean I don't understand your gender."

"Uh, yes"—he extends his pointer finger in the air—"it does."

"Oh, yeah?" I reply, grabbing hold of his finger. Eric

144

then grabs hold of my other hand and begins twisting as we both start laughing, "Hey! No fair using the moves you've learned watching the Wide World of Wrestling all these years."

"If it weren't for what I've learned from TV wrasslin', I wouldn't know nuthin' at all."

Because we're both now focused on our wrestling match that's playing out above our lunch bags, neither one of us notices that Natalie has approached our table until she pulls out the seat across from us and sits down.

"Hey," she says, causing both Eric and me to drop our hands immediately, both of us feeling like morons.

"Oh, hey," I reply.

Natalie nods to Eric, then says, "Hi, I'm Natalie."

"Eric," he replies.

"Oh, *this* is Eric! I've heard about you." Natalie smiles at me. "You're right, Grace, he is totally cute."

And somehow the moment just got more embarrassing still.

"Wait a second." Natalie cocks her head to the side. "Are you Eric Ward?"

"Yeah," he says.

"Oh, that makes sense!"

"What makes sense?"

"Well, your name came up. Let's just say Grace isn't the only one who's talking about you." She practically twinkles when she says this.

I've never had the impulse to ram a Ding Dong in

someone else's face before, but I'm quite certain that would take the glint out of Natalie's eye, at least temporarily. I watch as she brushes the hair that's fallen across her eyes off her face, and follow her hands as they fold across her waist.

Natalie sighs and leans in. "I just talked to Jake."

"Oh, really?" I try to sound blasé as I see Eric, who still looks a little uncomfortable, give me a conspiratorial smile.

"I told him I'm not going to go to the dance with him."

"That was a good decision." I nod.

"But here's the thing." Natalie idly clasps and unclasps the hook on her wristwatch. "I still really want to go. Are you guys going?" She looks between Eric and me.

We both kind of shrug, trying hard to avoid eye contact for the moment.

"I don't think so," Eric responds for the both of us, "we're not, like, typical dance people."

"Well, what's wrong with you two? They're so much fun!" she replies. "Wait, okay, I have this great idea, we three should go to the dance together."

"Oh, uh—" I hesitate.

"Um—" Eric says simultaneously.

"Excellent, I'll take those two eager responses as a yes." Natalie smiles. Then she pushes her chair out and stands up. "See you guys later! And practice up on your moves, because we're going to be out on the dance floor all night."

Eric and I sit there for a moment in silence after she's gone, then we both take a bite of our respective lunches and chew, mulling what's just happened and what it means.

At the very least it means that Eric and I will be going to the dance together after all.

♪ ♪ ♪

After explaining that I'd come down with a terrible twenty-four-hour virus, and was ready to make up the Vietnam test, my skeptical—but ultimately kind— American History teacher, Mr. Leightem, let me retake it after school. The questions were exactly the ones Eric and I had quizzed each other on, so for the first time in I don't know how long, I actually felt confident giving my answers. When I finished writing up a "working definition of *Vietnamization*," I handed my paper back to Mr. Leightem, and headed for home since today was one of my Hanover House off-days.

♪ ♪ ♪

Mom gets in from work around seven thirty, again looking like she'd been to war herself. "And how was your day?" I ask as she drops her bag and takes her shoes off by the door.

"Terrible. Refrigeration system broke in the restaurant on Lancaster Avenue."

"So all the food went bad?" I wonder if this makes

us the lucky recipients of a hundred pounds of almost spoiled ground chuck.

"Funny you should ask," Mom replies, plopping down to the couch. "The answer to that is no. And why not? Well, because Jim, the chief operating officer—the guy you'll recall I've had some issues with before—well, he thought this was a grand opportunity for us to have an impromptu 'all you can eat' promotion." Mom puts her hand on her forehead. "I thought for sure it was a joke, but no. So Peter not only had me trying to call in as much press as I could to promote it, he then insisted I help hostess in the restaurant to handle the overflow."

"You're kidding! You had to hostess?" I picture my mom wearing one of those awful You Say Potato . . . uniforms, and though part of me can't help thinking that it is sort of funny, the other part knows how horrible this would have to be for her.

"Do you believe that? I've worked there too long to have to put up with that shit." Anger flashes across her face. She'd started working in one of the chain's restaurants as a kitchen manager when Dad quit his job at the roofing company, and gradually worked her way up. That makes this return to in-restaurant work literally a move back down the food chain for her.

"Well, I hope you told them it was beneath your dignity," I say, suddenly feeling a wave of anger rising on her behalf. I look around our living room and realize it's a mess. After the day she had, I feel bad that Mom has to come home to this, so I start picking up the stray magazines and newspapers and making piles. "Hope you told him you wouldn't take it, Mom."

"Sure," she laughs, lying back on the couch, "and if I'd said that, he would have frog-marched me out the door."

"Well, just so you know, I'd be happy to go into that restaurant and tell him off for you if you want." I walk over to Mom at the couch and put my hand on her shoulder. "I mean, that's insane. You are just way too old to be hostessing!"

"Thanks, Grace," she replies, "that makes me feel much better."

"I mean—" I say quickly, "well you know what I mean."

"I do and I thank you anyway." Mom laughs again, then suddenly sits up and narrows her eyes at me. "Hey, what are you doing?"

"Just straightening up. You had a long day, and I just wanted to help out."

"Well, thanks again," she says, rubbing her feet. "You wouldn't want to take over the foot rubbing thing for me here, would you?"

"Um, gross."

"Worth a shot. You know what?" Mom says. "I don't really feel like cooking tonight, and I definitely didn't want to take any of the food home from work. What do you say we just order Chinese?"

"Good call." I pull the menu from the drawer in the kitchen by the phone and hand it to Mom. But even before I do, I know what she's going to order: egg drop soup and chicken in black bean sauce. Then she'll tell me to remind them to put in extra of those "crunchy things." But she surprises me tonight.

"I need red meat. This hot and spicy beef sounds good. And let's get a scallion pancake to start. What do you want?"

She needs red meat? Yikes.

"I'll get the chicken chow fun," I reply as I pick up the phone and dial the number for Hunan Pan.

"Is your sister around?" Mom asks, and when I shrug, she says, "Well, I suppose there'll be plenty left for her if she deigns to eat with us tonight." She smiles at me slyly. Lolly's let it be known that she's no longer talking to me, and though I don't think Mom knows exactly why Lolly's been so angry, she definitely knows something's up. I know she's not supposed to take sides, but especially tonight, I'm glad Mom's chosen mine. "Oh, and Grace, remind them to put in extra of those crunchy things."

"Of course." I smile back at her.

As Mom and I wait for the delivery guy, I sit down on the couch next to her. It's the first time that I can remember being in this position and not immediately reaching for the remote, but it wouldn't feel right.

"So Mom," I say, lifting her legs over my thighs so

she can still stay sprawled out on the couch, "what ever happened to that guy who owns the dry cleaner's next to the restaurant?" She'd mentioned his name a bunch of times recently, and I had a feeling it wasn't just because she was fond of the way he pressed her cuffs.

"Funny you should mention Tom," she says, a slight smile coming across her lips. "He's good. He actually came into the restaurant today."

"Not while you were hostessing?"

"Yes!" she replies, immediately growing more animated, almost teenagery. "I was mortified. I mean, can you imagine?"

"Mom, I'm a high school sophomore. Every day is that horror. What happened?"

"Well," she says, leaning toward me, "actually he was very sweet and he didn't make it awkward at all. He just said, 'To what do I owe this surprise? Such a lovely lady escorting me to my seat? Must be my lucky day!'"

"What did you say?" I ask.

"I told him that someone needed to set the example, and when I looked around the restaurant, I realized I was the only one qualified to do it!" Mom smiles broadly and I can tell she's still proud of herself for coming up with that line.

"Very nice!" What's strange is that I am genuinely pleased by my mom's response. Here she is telling me about the fact that she's flirting with a man who's not my dad, and I'm actually happy that she seems so happy. This is the first time we've ever had a conversation like this, but instead of tiptoeing around the subject, it feels like we're both hungry to have it. "So do you know Tom's deal yet? I mean, is he dateable?"

Mom rolls her eyes. "I don't know," she says quickly. "I think he's a few years younger than me and I don't think he has any kids, so . . ."

It never occurred to me that two teenage daughters might not be the best accessory to have on a first date. Lolly and I are like two strikes against Mom. We're the equivalent of two big zits on her nose and forehead, but worse because we never go away. I'd never thought about how lonely she must feel sometimes. "Well, are you going to make the first move?"

"Definitely not. What would that get me?"

"Dinner and a movie?"

"I'm telling you. They might be interested in you for a little while if you're really forward—especially if you're putting out for them—which, heaven forbid you're doing," Mom says. "But once they've had their fill, they'll just split. I hate to say it, but all that stuff they try to tell you about women being empowered and about how it's fine for a woman to ask a man out, well, it's crap."

I look down at my watch. "Seven fifty-three p.m."

"What does that mean?"

"Official time of death of feminism," I reply, and Mom laughs, but my mind drifts to Eric, and how I was the one who kissed him first. From what Isabelle said and from what Mom has just implied, I'm already screwed.

"Believe me," she says, "I wish that weren't the case. I've just tried the other way enough times to learn a thing or two about human nature. So how's your friend Eric?" A smile comes across her face like she knows something.

I'd never had any intention of telling my mother what had been going on between Eric and me, but since she does have all this experience, I'm kind of curious to get her opinion on the situation. "*Well,* things have been a little weird between us, but he did ask me to go to the school dance with him."

"Really?" she replies. "That's exciting."

"Yes and no."

"What does that mean?"

"The only reason he wants to go is so he can hang out with the upperclassmen on the basketball team." What I really want to hear is for Mom to defend me against . . . myself. I need her to tell me that that's *not* the reason Eric asked me to the dance.

"Ouch," she says instead.

I shrug. "Anyway, it's not like I have anything to wear if I did go. I'd probably need to get a new outfit because I've outgrown any fancy stuff I ever owned." Now it would be nice for me to hear something like "Oh, honey, you'll be the best-looking girl at the dance regardless of what you're wearing."

"It does seem like a waste to spend good money on a new dress when you're just being brought along as 'the friend.'" Mom raises her eyebrows, and her forehead creases into a series of raised rows and trenches. "Maybe Lolly would loan you one of her old dresses."

"Yeah okay, *thanks*, Mom. That's *exactly* what I want." Showing up in my sister's reject clothes. As if I don't already feel like enough of a reject already.

"Hey, I'm not the enemy here," Mom replies, sounding like I'm the one who offended *her*.

"I'm sorry I brought it up."

"Grace, don't be like this," she calls after me as I head for the stairs.

"Don't be like this?" I repeat, stopping in my tracks. "How do you think I got this way in the first place? Ever think that maybe if I had some decent role models I wouldn't be so messed up? I might even have a fighting chance at being normal?" I storm up to my room, dizzied by how quickly the tears spring to my eyes. It's like they've been waiting right there in the corners, ready to roll at a moment's notice. Ready to wash down and flood out the anger, frustration, sadness, confusion, and all the rest of the crap that's floating through my head.

Chapter Twelve

I find Isabelle still sitting in Mr. Sands's room when I drop in during my Tuesday shift, and I have a bad feeling. She doesn't look like she's moved since the last time I spied her here. She glances up when I enter.

"Grace!" she says, smiling at me, then looking back to Mr. Sands. "Frank, Grace is here. I didn't think you came in today!"

I don't want to make her feel bad for mixing up the days, so I just smile and say, "I wanted to come say hello." I start walking toward the bed, waiting for Mr. Sands to say something witty about his gathering harem. But he doesn't respond. "He sleeping?" I whisper.

Isabelle looks down at her hands and shakes her head. "No, he's just . . . well, he's having some difficulty speaking today."

Over the past several weeks I'd noticed Mr. Sands's voice had been more nasal-sounding and he'd been slurring his words with more frequency, but even though I knew losing the ability to speak was one of the symptoms of his disease, I couldn't really believe it would happen . . . That it *was* happening.

"Will he be able to speak again?" I ask her, almost ignoring the fact that Mr. Sands is still in the room with us.

"Oh, I'm sure he will, won't you, Frank?" Isabelle says, rubbing her hand against his shoulder. But I can't tell if she said that because it's really true, whether it was for his benefit or mine.

Mr. Sands grunts and rolls his eyes, sending a pretty clear signal that he's not only very much still present, but also quite capable of expressing his opinion despite today's difficulty with words.

"So tell us, Grace, how was your day?" Isabelle asks, and I can tell she wants me to carry the conversation for a while. "What's going on with your friend Eric? Have you seen him play in any basketball games yet?"

"Actually, his first game's tonight," I reply.

"How exciting!"

"I guess," I say, pulling two chairs around from the back of the room so Isabelle and I can both sit down. "But things have gotten a little weird between Eric and me, so I'm not really sure I should go. I don't want to be a distraction or anything."

"Hmm," she replies. "That sounds like utter nonsense to me, what do you think, Frank?"

Mr. Sands doesn't make a sound, but he closes his eyes, which we both take as assent.

"Yeah, but see we . . ." I'm too self-conscious to explain what happened in Eric's room the other night.

"Wait! Wait! Don't tell me. Did you do this?" Isabelle

asks, leaning over Mr. Sands and kissing him lightly on the lips.

When I nod, she giggles. My mortification is now complete.

"I had a feeling that would get Frank's attention," she says. "Okay, so what happened after that?"

"Well, Eric wanted to talk about it when I saw him in school. But I said if we just pretended like the whole thing never happened, we could just go back to the way things were."

"You didn't really say that, did you?" Isabelle replies with a laugh.

"Why, was that bad?"

"No," she says at first, then quickly adds, "Actually, yes. Well, it just sounds like something I would have said myself," Isabelle replies. "But that thing you're trying to avoid by burying your head in the sand? It'll sit right next to you, waiting for you to come up to take a breath. And when you do, you'll realize it's only gotten bigger and won't leave your side until you deal with it."

As Isabelle Sands says this, I keep my eyes on her husband lying there next to her. I can't help thinking about his request for "help." If he asked Isabelle, how did she react? What did she say? Did she think his life wasn't hers to take away? Did she worry she'd be charged with murder? Or maybe Mr. Sands couldn't bring himself to ask his wife . . .

Looking at Mr. Sands, present but silent, here but

not here, it's impossible to ignore what's happening to him now: the thing he most feared.

"Nothing exactly feels normal anymore," I confess. "I'm trying my hardest to make things seem fine, but there's all this stuff hanging in the air."

Isabelle nods. "Do you know what Eric's thinking about all this?"

"Not really. I mean, he might even be interested in this other girl at school—or a couple of other girls at school—but I'm not sure."

Isabelle pats my hand. "Well then, aren't you lucky this happened between you and your best friend and not just some random fellow you met on the bus?"

"Lucky? Lucky how? If this had happened between me and some random guy, I wouldn't care. But because it's Eric, I do care. I *really* care."

"Well, there you have it." She smiles. "You *'really'* care for him. Seems to me that's the best foundation for a relationship you can have, no? If I've learned anything from my years with Frank it's that relationships are hard. Isn't that right, honey?" Isabelle strokes Frank's arm, and we both watch him breathe for a moment. "Life just has a way of throwing all sorts of curveballs. But if you truly care about the well-being of the other person, eventually you'll find the way to do right by them." Isabelle adds softly, "I hope we're doing right by Frank here."

"Yeah." I nod. "I hope so . . . You think there's any way to know that for sure?"

Isabelle exhales and I look away from her, wondering if she's thinking about the same thing I am—whether it's doing right to allow someone to languish.

॰ॐ ॐ ॐ

I find Lolly sprawled out on her bedroom floor when I get home later that afternoon. I'd been so much in my own head today, I hadn't given any thought to the fact I hadn't seen her at school. Though it isn't uncommon for us to pass each other in the halls without speaking, it is weird not to see her at all . . . which makes me wonder if she was there . . . which makes me wonder if hiding out is a Manning family trait. "Hey, everything okay?" I ask as I pass by her door.

"Not really," she replies. "You want to come in for a minute?"

"Yeah, okay, sure." I walk in and awkwardly stand over my sister for a moment, before I realize I should probably join her on the floor. I flop down and cross my legs, yet still feel like I'm hovering above Lolly. She looks even smaller to me than she did yesterday.

"What's wrong with them, Grace? Why are all guys so screwed up?"

The question catches me off guard. I'd been so focused on other things, it takes a moment for me to change the mental channel. "Um, I'm not sure *all* guys are screwed up," I reply, trying to return to her wavelength. "Just most of the ones we seem to know."

"I don't understand why he had to be *such* an ass, though, you know? I mean, the way he played both me and Natalie? He's such a jerk. Is she really upset too?"

Now is not the time to tell Lolly that Jake didn't play Natalie, it was more like the other way around. "I think she's just disgusted by him."

"You were right. I know you've always had this thing about him, but before now I just thought it was because you were jealous."

"Jealous of Jake?" I'd never given that idea any thought, but now that she mentions it, maybe I was. As soon as he came into the picture, it seemed like all of her energy was taken up by him. I guess I *was* jealous.

"No, jealous of me!" She laughs. "I thought you had a crush on him."

"Ha! Uh, no, Lolly, that was never an issue."

"Well, okay I see that now." She rolls her eyes. "You always knew he was a jerk, didn't you?"

I nod. "I could see how you would think he was cute, though."

"He is cute, right?"

"I actually meant that in the 'some people think giant ferrets are cute and I don't understand that either' type of way, but I get that everyone has her own taste—weird as it may be. But thinking he'd be a good boyfriend? No, that never crossed my mind. You were always too good for him."

"Really? What makes you say that?"

I can't tell her this is a recurring line I've heard on Lifetime that always seems to make the heroine feel better. "First of all," I reply, trying to think quickly, "you're much too pretty for him."

"Shut up," she says, obviously wanting to hear more.

"Really, Lolly, you're great-looking." Lolly is pretty. Great-looking is a stretch, but it's what she needs to hear right now, and though I'm no expert on morality, I'm pretty sure this type of "truth stretching" can't be a bad thing.

"Am I as pretty as Natalie?" she asks.

"She's just more 'traditional' American pie pretty, you know? You've got your own thing going on."

"Grace, you know you have the potential to be really good-looking yourself." Lolly sits up as I react, blinking back the insult. "No, I didn't mean it to be mean! You have a really pretty face, I just meant you should take care of yourself a little more. You're always eating crap. It's going to make you fat and ruin your skin."

"Maybe I like to eat crap?"

"So does everyone," Lolly responds, shaking her head. "But let's be honest: When Dad left, you went looking for him at the bottom of a Doritos bag."

"So if that's the thing that somehow makes me feel a little better, is that so wrong?"

Lolly reaches for my arm. "Yes," she says with a nod. "You know why?" I turn away from her and don't respond, but this doesn't stop her from talking. "Because all the junk food in the world isn't going to make Dad come back."

I stay silent. This was *not* the conversation I was prepared to have this afternoon. The most maddening thing about it is that some small part of me knows that Lolly (Lolly!) might be right.

"Look, Grace, I didn't mean to upset you. I just want things to start feeling better for both of us. I mean, even if you just started wearing clothes that flatter you more, I think it would be a start."

"Trust me when I tell you this is not the time to hit Mom up for a new wardrobe," I say with a laugh, deciding to let the anger go.

"I know." Lolly nods. "Though when *is* the right time for that? I asked her for a new sports bra since I outgrew my last one and she looked at me as if I'd just asked her to buy me a pony."

I can picture the exact expression Mom must have given Lolly, and I do my best impersonation of it, which makes Lolly laugh again.

"Hey, want me to do your makeup?" she asks.

"Makeup?" No.

"Come on, it'll be fun. Go sit on the bed." Lolly walks over to her bureau, then carries her three-tiered makeup chest back towards me.

"You've got a lot of stuff in there." I eye the chest. "How do you even know what goes where? Or is that like

162

a natural thing that a person has to be born with?"

"Practice," she says, squeezing brownish goop into her hands before rubbing it into my cheeks and forehead. "Hey, have you been coloring your hair?"

I'm not sure whether to admit to this or not. Mom will go nuts if she ever finds out, and I don't kid myself to think that my relationship with Lolly will be forever changed after tonight. But right now I am feeling closer to her than I have in a long time, and there's something really nice about that. "Yep." I nod.

"I knew it," she replies. "You've been doing it since right around your birthday, haven't you?"

"Yeah but don't—" I start to say, but Lolly cuts me off.

"Come on, Grace, I'm not going to tell on you. I'm your sister." And that's all she has to say.

♪ ♪ ♪

Later that night I convince Lolly to come see Eric's basketball game with me. She was worried that Jake would be there, but I told her she'd have to face him eventually, and since we'd spent so long getting the makeup right this afternoon, this would be as good a face to show him as any. The logic made sense to her, which was a relief to me because I wanted to go to the game to support Eric, but I didn't want to sit in the stands all dolled up and Han Solo.

When we arrive, the school parking lot is jammed. "What's going on here?" I ask.

"Do you even go to this school?" Lolly replies. "This is a big game, Grace—Harriton vs. Lower Merion—our rival school, remember?"

I hadn't remembered the night's matchup. At that point I was glad I could even remember the name of my own high school. When Lolly and I walk into the gym, I see Eric dribbling the ball back and forth across center court with Mike Richter, and I can't help but smile seeing him in that uniform. It's not just that the shorts are slightly longer on him than the rest of his taller teammates, it's more that he's wearing a uniform in the first place. I consider trying to catch his attention, but I don't want to distract or embarrass him, so I just keep my eyes on him as I let Lolly find us the spot where she wants to sit.

"So, is Eric going to start?" Lolly asks as we move through the crowded middle of the risers.

I shrug my shoulders. "Dunno."

"You're a good friend," she laughs, sitting down on the wooden bench.

"What's that supposed to mean?"

Lolly raises her eyebrows, surprised that I'm surprised. "Well, you are his *best* friend, right? I just assumed that's something you guys would have talked about."

As soon as she says it, I know Lolly has a point. Whether or not Eric started was something we definitely *would have* talked about in our normal conversations.

But recently our conversations have felt anything but normal. "Well, he's just been at practice a lot and I don't think the coach had made any final decisions about the lineup or anything."

"Grace," she says, "some advice: Act interested. Even if you're not, *try* to act interested. If you don't, trust me, a lot of the other girls in this school will . . . if they haven't already." Lolly tips her head courtside, and when I look over I see Chelsea Roy on the sidelines. She's managed to catch Mike's and Eric's attention, and though they're still passing the ball back and forth to each other, they're also carrying on a conversation with her. About something *really* important, I'm sure.

"Ew, could she be any more obvious?"

"If she could, I'm sure she'd find a way, Gracie," Lolly replies. "And that's exactly what I'm talking about."

I don't dignify this with a response, mainly because I don't have one, so I keep watching their conversation instead. A minute later I decide that I might as well go over to say hello, but when I turn to Lolly to tell her I'll be right back, I see her staring at her own fixed point in the crowd. Jake's sitting a few risers away, surrounded by his group of guy friends, *his boys*. Thankfully there are no girls sitting with them, but I get the feeling their absence doesn't make Lolly feel any better. I stick my hand in my coat pocket and pull out a half-eaten Milky Way.

"You want the rest?" I say, tapping the candy bar wrapper against her knee. "You could eat it from the other side."

Lolly looks down and wrinkles her nose. "That's okay, thanks," she says.

"No, you're right," I reply, rewrapping the Milky Way and shoving it back into my pocket, embarrassed by the offering. I keep my hand in my coat and wrap my fist around the candy bar, giving it a firm squeeze and enjoy feeling it smoosh between my fingers. When I look back to the court again and see Chelsea smile and wave good-bye to Eric and Mike as she turns and heads for the stands, I clutch the candy bar a little tighter.

Eric does not start for the team. Still, he is subbed in during the first quarter.

"The coach must think he's pretty decent to play him this early," Lolly says with approval. "Usually they only play the little guys when the team is either so far ahead or so far behind, they can't have any effect on the outcome."

"That must build confidence," I reply, not taking my eyes off Eric as he runs back and forth on the court. As far as I can tell, he's not really doing very much, and the guy he's guarding has about half a foot and thirty pounds on him. But he's giving his all. I'm not sure if what I'm feeling is pride—that it's *my* Eric who's in the middle of the action—or whether it's just general excitement for my friend, but I can feel the adrenaline coursing through my body as he runs up and down the court.

Though I expected Harriton to take a beating from its bitter and better rival, the team is doing surprisingly well. The score bounces back and forth throughout the night, and the gym thunders with the crowd's excited cheers. Harriton's coach continues rotating his players. When Eric and Mike are out on the court together, they both play well, and the time they spent practicing with each other is clearly paying off.

"Little Eric Ward, who would have guessed!" Lolly says, leaning over to me as the Harriton side stands to do the wave. "Not bad at all."

"Taught him everything he knows," I reply, throwing my arms over my head.

"No doubt." She smiles, lowering her arms and sitting back down again.

With a minute and a half left in the game, Eric is still on the court. Intercepting the ball, Eric quickly turns it around and throws the ball back to Mike. The two make their way to the midfield and as the shot clock winds down, Mike passes back to Eric, who goes for the long shot. Hurtling through the air, the ball miraculously swishes through the basket for the three-pointer with a minute to go in the game. The Harriton side goes wild. We are up by two when the game ends. We win! We actually win.

"Wow," I say, turning to Lolly, "are basketball games usually this exciting?"

"No," she replies, looking off in Jake's direction, "usually they suck."

"Eric was good, wasn't he? I'm going to go over and congratulate him. You want to come?"

Lolly keeps staring at Jake and I know what she really wants is for him to come over here, confess he's been an idiot and experienced temporary insanity, and beg her forgiveness. "You go ahead," she says.

"Come on," I reply, dragging her with me.

When we get down to the court, a lot of kids are milling around, happy for the chance to celebrate and not yet ready to go home. Eric's standing in a group of a few players, but I catch his eye as Lolly and I approach.

"Hey!" I say as Eric turns from the guys to greet me. Lolly pushes me forward, not so subtly letting me know that I should hug him, which I not so subtly do, wrapping my arms around Eric and quickly giving him an awkward squeeze. This is something we'll definitely need to work on if it's ever going to feel natural.

"You made it," he says, smiling. "I looked for you in the stands, but I didn't see you."

"Are you kidding? I wouldn't have missed your star turn."

"It was a pretty good game, huh?" he replies.

"You were terrific."

"Hey, kiddo, great game!" Eric's mom says. "Hi Grace."

"Hi, Mrs. Ward, hi Mr. Ward," I reply as Eric's dad strides over and nods at me.

"Nice shot, son," he says, pawing Eric's head.

"Thanks, Dad," he says. Then, turning to Mike, he says, "But this is the guy who made it all possible." Giant Mike smiles and waves down to all of us, clapping Eric's hand in a high five.

"Ohmigod, Eric!" Chelsea Roy runs up and throws her arms around him. "You were awesome," she trills. When she breaks the hug, she bumps her hip against Mike. "Both of you guys were!" I watch for a moment as the boys beam under Chelsea's praise. But the Chelsea effect is diminished as soon as Natalie approaches the group.

"Eric," Natalie says, smiling at him, pink glossed lips parted slightly to reveal perfectly shaped, straight white teeth. "Amazing." She touches his elbow and keeps her hand there for a moment before letting go. That's all she says before she turns and walks away, but the boys' eyes trail after her as she moves through the crowd. Once Natalie's out of view, their circle closes back around Eric, Mike, Chelsea, and Eric's parents; Lolly and I are on the outside. I stand there for another minute, waiting to be reabsorbed, but as they continue to chat, I begin to feel more and more on the wrong side of the ring. "Come on," I say to Lolly, "let's go." I manage to tap Eric's arm and get his attention. "Lolly and I are going to take off," I say.

"Okay, see ya," he replies.

"Yeah." I nod. "And congrats," I add as he turns his attention back to his fans. I glance at Lolly to get her take on what just happened, but she's looking down and appears sullen, so I just link arms with my sister and we head for the exit.

When we get home, I grab the tube of slice and bake cookies from the freezer and go to my room. I push up on the raw dough and squeeze it out like toothpaste on my index finger as I lie on top of my bed and stare at the ceiling. *"Any thoughts?"*

No response.

"I know. I know. I didn't deal and now I may have permanently screwed things up with Eric. And by holding my breath for Mr. Sands—hoping for a miracle instead of doing something—I may be adding to his pain. But if I help him to die, will I be able to live with myself? Or is that something I'd regret doing as long as I live?"

Ultimately the big question seems to be this: What do you do when you realize "hoping for the best" is a losing strategy?

Chapter Thirteen

As I'm getting dressed for school I think about Lolly's advice, and instead of putting on a T-shirt and sweats, I take the nice black V-neck sweater that I got for Christmas—a cashmere blend, as Mom repeated several times—out of my drawer and pair it with my best-fitting jeans. I still might not be a fashion plate, but it's a better look than normal.

Eric's standing by his locker when I get to school, so I walk over as he finishes talking with guy next to him.

"Hey," I say, "hope you're still getting props on your performance last night."

"What?" Eric replies, distracted.

"The game? Your three-pointer? Don't tell me you're so cool that you've already forgotten it?"

"Oh, yeah, no. I mean thanks," he says. "I just don't want people thinking it was such a big deal because I don't want them to think I'm always going to be able to pull off a shot like that."

"Yeah." I nod. "That'd be the worst. People constantly talking about how good you are and the great expectations they have for you."

Eric smiles. "I just hope it wasn't a fluke."

"Of course it wasn't a fluke!" I say, leaning against a locker. "You're really good and I'm sorry, but you're just going to have to live with that fact."

"Thanks," Eric replies, but from the jumpiness of his eyes and the fact that he won't seem to hold my gaze, I get the feeling that there's more here. That something else is going on.

"Okay, what's with your face?"

"What do you mean?" Eric runs his hand over his jaw.

"I mean I can see something's bouncing around in that head of yours."

"Un-uh," he replies.

"I know that look, and I've known you too long for you to deny it."

Eric runs his left hand under his nose a few times.

"And there's your tell," I say.

"What?"

"Mr. Sands taught me that when people are trying to bluff at poker, they almost always give some sort of sign that they're doing it. It's unconscious, of course, but almost everyone has one. It's as if we're not really programmed to lie, so our conscience betrays us. That nose wipe is your tell. You did it right after you denied something was up. So why don't you just tell me what you're trying to hide and it'll save both of us a lot of time."

"Okay." Eric shakes his head, knowing he's busted. "Well, as I was leaving the gym last night, Natalie was driving by in the parking lot and offered to give me a ride home."

"Well, that's weird. I mean, she knew your parents were there."

"Yeah, I know, we were even walking to our car together when she stopped. But my dad had left something at the office and needed to stop downtown first, so he kind of encouraged me to go with her," he says quickly, making eye contact and then looking away.

"Okay . . ." I feel the knots in my stomach start to tighten.

"Anyway," Eric continues, "we're driving and she's just talking about the game and stupid school stuff, and the whole time I'm wondering what's going on. Why is Natalie Talbot giving me a ride a home? And then I remember that conversation we had in the cafeteria when she said that weird thing about how you weren't the only one talking about me. What did you say to her, Grace?"

Oh my god, I made this happen.

"I didn't say anything, really," I say, "just might have told her you thought she was pretty or something. So what happened?"

"Well, so when we pull into my driveway, she just puts the car in park, like she's not going anywhere for a while. Then she starts saying all this stuff about how nobody really understands her, how people seemed to have this image of her that isn't who she is."

"She didn't try the whole 'no one thinks I'm pretty thing' did she?" When Eric nods, I swallow hard. "Well, what did you do? Did you tell her it wasn't true? Wait, wait! Did you reassure her that you think she's 'the prettiest girl in school.' What was it? Or 'the prettiest girl in school. By. Far.'"

"Not exactly those words, no. But I told her I thought she was cute, yeah." Eric shifts on his feet. "Then she goes, 'Prove it.'"

"Uhm, what?" I crook my leg and put my foot against the locker wanting to look like I'm coolly handling the news. Which I'm not. "What did you do?"

"Nothing. I didn't do anything," he says, and I feel my body relax. "The whole thing seemed so bizarre, I was half convinced the guys on the team had set it up and there was some sort of video camera running. I mean especially when she leaned over and . . ." He trails off and shrugs.

"And what? *What?* What does that mean?"

"Grace, I don't think we should be talking about this."

"You can tell me," I say, needing to know *and what.* "You're the one who likes to talk, right?"

Eric looks profoundly uncomfortable. "She started kissing me and stuff, okay?"

And stuff.

"And did you kiss her 'and stuff' back?" I stare at him, but Eric looks to the ground.

"Grace, what do you want me to say?"

"Natalie Talbot. Well, good for you," I reply, shaking my head and turning away, yet again unable to express my true thoughts.

♪ ♪ ♪

I don't want to be alone this afternoon. If I am, I know I won't be able to get the image of Eric kissing Natalie out of my head. So I head to Hanover House even though it's not my assigned day. I go directly to Mr. Sands's room, hoping I'll find Isabelle there too, so I can just listen to her tell more stories about their relationship. But Isabelle isn't in Mr. Sands's room when I get there after school, and when I walk in, I see that he's hooked to another machine now, a tube running into his mouth.

"Hi, Mr. Sands, it's Grace," I say, approaching him like I've done so many times in the past.

His eyes flutter open and he blinks at me several times.

"Well, thank you for noticing. I *do* look nice today, don't I?" I smile. "Dressed up just for you."

Mr. Sands winks with his left eye. Despite what he's going through I'm pretty sure that he's calling me out on the lie. Just like he's done so many times in the past.

"Okay, so maybe it wasn't *entirely* for you that I put on pants that buttoned," I say. "But you seem to be the only one who appreciates it."

"Good afta-noon, Mr. Frank," Nurse Victoria says, charging into the room, pulling a cart loaded with medical devices behind her. "Grace," she says with a nod in my direction. "I hafta take some blood, check your pressure, and oh, ya drooling again! Well, let's take care of that first." Victoria pulls a small device off the cart, holds the base of the unit in her left hand and its straw-like tube in her right. She inserts the tube in Mr. Sands's mouth and the unmistakable dentist's office sound of a gurgling saliva vacuum fills the air. "Can ya cough for me, Mr. Frank?" He does his best, but even this natural reflex seems like a challenge. "That's fine," she says, "just want ta make sure we're getting as much of that phlegm as we can."

"Should I go?" I ask Victoria, hoping she'll excuse me from observing the rest of their routine.

"No, ya don't need ta." She puts the suction machine back on the cart and takes a washcloth to Mr. Sands's face to mop the drool that had previously escaped. "Won't be here too much longer. Just need to measure tha sugar." Victoria lifts Mr. Sands's left hand and pricks his middle finger to draw a drop of blood. "And how's the other hand feeling today?" she asks, lifting his right arm from the bed. There's a practiced swiftness to her actions, which makes Victoria's sudden but perceptible reaction to the condition of his right hand all the more surprising.

I look from Victoria to Mr. Sands's hand, now seeing

what she does: Mr. Sands's fingers have curled into a claw. Gently, Victoria tries to move the fingers apart, but from the moan Mr. Sands manages to emit, it's clear this is a painful procedure.

"Okay, Mr. Frank," she says compassionately, resting the hand back down on the bed. "I'm sorry about that. I'm not trying to hurt ya. Just trying to see what we're dealing with here. Now I'm gonna have a look at those nice legs of yours." Victoria smiles at him as she lifts the sheet covering Mr. Sands's legs, and I consider looking away to give some semblance of privacy, but I can't after glimpsing what look like legs that seem to belong to two different people. The left is substantially bigger than the right, swollen I suppose, and the color is different too. The upper thigh of his left leg is also much redder than its mate. Victoria nods. "I'm going to ask Dr. Baker to come by," she says, trying not to sound troubled by what we both see. "I think he should have a look at this." Victoria puts her hand on my shoulder, then gathers her equipment back on the cart and walks out, leaving us alone again.

Mr. Sands blinks rapidly several times, but I can't decipher the code. What I can read though is his look of discomfort; his *dis-ease*. It's the look of a man forced to endure his worst fear.

I sit against the side of his bed since it seems like it'll be easier to "talk" to him at closer range.

It isn't.

"This is hard, isn't it?"

Mr. Sands closes his eyes for a long second, then opens them, effectively communicating the words: "No shit, Sherlock."

I break his stare and look out the window, not wanting to see him when I ask the next question: "It's going to get worse still, isn't it?"

Mr. Sands takes an exaggerated breath, reminding me that in the last stages of this disease, you can't even breathe—the most basic life function—on your own either. I think Mr. Sands would turn away from me now if he could, because that's when he starts crying. It seems the tears rolling down his cheeks are the only part of his body that can flow so easily.

My eyes well and I wipe off my face with the back of my sleeve, knowing how much he's suffering.

"Mr. Sands, do you still want . . ." I can't quite get it out.

Mr. Sands blinks slowly, then he blinks again. Summoning what's probably the last reserve of his strength, he moves his body a bit on the bed.

"That's a yes? Just blink once if that's a yes."

Mr. Sands blinks once, then stares into my eyes.

That's the signal, the clear sign that tells me I need to do right for my friend. Before my head can even process what my gut and heart already know, I'm in motion. No one will know it was me. I walk to the nightstand and reach far back into the drawer where I'd left my report card envelope containing his pills. No one will suspect the fifteen-year-old candy striper. Then I take the envelope out of the drawer and stick it in the back pocket of my jeans. It will all seem natural.

"I'll be back," I say. "I'll help you."

✧ ✧ ✧

I pull ingredients from the refrigerator and kitchen shelves in a frenzy: flour, sugar, eggs, milk, salt, and baking powder. But as I'm putting my hands on an old jug of pancake syrup that we'd ordered from a special online gourmet shop, I flash to images of Mr. Sands's dinner trays. Over the course of the last few weeks, the food on those trays went from "solids" (chicken, pasta, fish) to "softs" (mashed potatoes, smashed peas, beef purees) to "shakes" (cans of high protein and nutrient-rich glop). And a terrible thought occurs to me: Mr. Sands probably won't be able to chew the pancake if I make it for him.

Maybe it's a sign?

I push the chair back under the kitchen table and start mulling this when Lolly walks in, her cardigan ridiculously misbuttoned. Even with all the other things on my mind, I can't help but laugh. "Please tell me you went through school like that," I say, and nod my head in the direction of the button fiasco.

"What?" Oblivious, Lolly glances down, "Oh, shit. Glad Mom didn't catch me looking like this!"

"Does that mean you were with Jake?"

"Don't make a big deal of this, Grace," she says.

"Which means what?"

"Look." Lolly lowers her voice and comes over to the kitchen table. "Jake and I talked after school and he told me what a huge mistake he'd made by breaking up with me. He told me how sorry he was and he asked me if I could forgive him. He was really upset. I mean, how could I say no?"

"By saying no." I'm trying to hold back from telling her that the only reason he came crawling back was because Natalie dumped him—for Eric. "I don't get it, Lol. You're forgiving him just because he asked you? You know you don't have to do everything people ask because it makes *them* feel better." When I make a sweeping motion with my hand, it accidentally knocks the bag of flour and a puff of white powder is released in the air. As I watch the particles fall, I realize what I've just said and wonder what circle of hell is reserved for hypocrites.

"Oh, like you've never done anything wrong? Like you've never needed to be forgiven anything because you're perfect. Right, Grace?"

"No, that's not what I mean," I say softly, looking around at the ingredients I've gathered.

"Seriously, what gives *you* the right to judge me?"

Lolly's words stick in my chest. She shakes her head at me, grabs a Diet Coke from the fridge, and walks out of the kitchen.

Of course I have no right to judge her, and the crazy thing is, I also know on some level, *the words* Lolly said made some sense: People do screw up. They constantly fall for all sorts of scams and plots, they act only according to their own best interest (often at the expense of others). They make mistakes big and small—sometimes even when they think they're doing right. And it *would* be terrible to think that we can't be forgiven for our errors.

I start thinking about that story on the news a long time ago. There had been this convict in Atlanta who escaped from a courthouse and went on a killing spree, terrorizing people in the city for a few days. He finally wound up taking this woman hostage, and randomly she turned out to be someone who'd had some encounters with the law herself. She'd had a drug problem, the father of her child had been stabbed to death in a bar brawl, and she'd been in mental institutions repeatedly. Anyway, when the fugitive guy started talking to this woman, whom he'd tied up on her bed with an extension cord, she starts telling him about her life. And she tells him that she's been trying to find the purpose in her life through God. She even starts reading to him from this book about God, and she later said that her reading helped calm him down. The woman actually manages to convince this cold-blooded killer to surrender. She's a hero, no question about it, even if the details of her life to that point never would have indicated it.

But the most interesting part of this story for me only came out a few months later, when the book she's written about the drama is about to be released. She admits then that this felon guy had asked her if she had any marijuana and she said no, because she didn't. What she did have, though—and what she gave to him—was crystal meth. Now whether you believe it was actually the meth that ultimately calmed this guy down and made him docile enough to surrender to the police, or whether it was, in fact, that she spoke to him about God's plan—well, I think that probably depends on how you were raised. But to me, it really doesn't matter. She had those drugs, which would have made her technically a sinner both in the eyes of the church and in the eyes of the law. But it's just possible that it was *only* because she had those drugs—only because she really was a "sinner" herself—that she was able to get through to this guy.

I like the story because it proves it's not just perfect people who do good, heroic things. Heroism is a choice. It's about making a hard decision—often without regard to how it'll affect you personally—and then following through on it. Being heroic means you don't take the easy way out; you take action because you know in your heart it's the right thing to do. And I don't know if I'll ever be in a position where I'll need to be heroic like that woman was, but it's nice to know that I haven't been disqualified yet. It's nice to know that I could. That I can.

♪ ♪ ♪

They lock the front door at Hanover House at 9:00 p.m., but from the time Mr. Sands and I stole out on our little adventure, I know about the side entrance. I also know the nurses tend to keep it unlocked so they can sneak in and out for smoke breaks. I wait until just past 11:00 to head back to Hanover House, putting the envelope of pills, the small jug of syrup, and a spoon in my book bag. I know I'm going to have to dissolve the pills in water and have him drink the bitter cocktail, but if Mr. Sands can't go out eating cake as he wanted, at least he can have the sweet taste of syrup on his tongue.

I ride down the near-empty streets and ditch my bike near the door, not bothering to lock it. I don't want to risk being seen stashing it on the bike rack up front.

I can't get caught, I repeat to myself partially as a mantra and partially as a warning. *I can't get caught.*

Just as I assumed, when I try the side door handle it opens, and I walk down the corridor of the most gravely ill patients. A strong smell of antiseptic from the nightly cleaning crew's work stings my nose, and I'm aware of the dull sounds of machines beeping and whirring in the background. I usually don't hear them during the daytime when the area's full of people. I look at the names of the residents on these doors. They're written with Sharpies on pieces of white medical tape—just rip the tape off and the room's ready for its next victim. It's like they're not even bothering to pretend these people will be here next week.

The hallway is empty and I slip into Mr. Sands's room.

This is insane! What am I doing?

"Mr. Sands," I say in a low whisper. "Mr. Sands," I say again, leaning hard against his arm to rouse him. He stirs, and his eyelids flutter. "I'm here." His eyes close again. "You told me you were ready," I whisper. "This *is* what you want, right?"

He doesn't say no.

He doesn't say yes.

He lies there, no longer the man who always had the answers to my questions. Now he can't even answer the most basic one. I feel sick to my stomach. *Will this even work? . . . Worse: What if it does?*

I take the envelope of pills out of my book bag and put it down on the windowsill before crushing my palm into it, breaking the pills into littler pieces. It might be more effective if I just stepped on the envelope and crunched the pills with my foot, but that seems disrespectful. As I'm crushing the contents of the envelope, I see a photo taped to the guardrail on his bed that I'd never noticed before. It's a wallet-sized wedding photo of Isabelle and him. He's in a white dinner jacket and black bow tie. She's in a long, column-like white gown, the train bustled at her feet. They're looking into each other's eyes promising till death do them part, but in this picture they are immortal.

I can't do this. I can't kill Mr. Sands. Isabelle's husband. My friend.

I can't help him die. Even if he wants to.

How would I live with myself? How would I live with the guilt?

I look from the picture back to the bed. But the man in the bed is not the same man as the one in the picture. And the man in the picture wouldn't recognize himself either. The man frozen in the picture would say the man frozen on the bed has no quality of life.

There's a pitcher of water at the end of the bed and two plastic cups stacked next to it, the kind they serve you juice in when you're in kindergarten. As I eyeball the cups, a geometry problem suddenly occurs to me—an actual real problem concerning volume. I can see the cups are not big enough to hold the water it'll take to dissolve the pills.

I need to get a bigger cup, but where am I going to get it? I could go to the cafeteria . . . but if I did that, there's a chance someone might see me. It's just too risky to get caught on the premises now because Mr. Sands was right, no one will have any reason to suspect my involvement unless I do something boneheaded like being seen here—after hours, near his room—the night he dies. Maybe I could use only half of the pills . . . but what if that's not enough to do the job? I couldn't bear the idea of having to come back and do this again . . . or leaving him even worse off than he is now. Which leaves me with the only other possibility: I'm going to have to use both of the cups. I'm going to have to do this twice.

I fill up one of the cups three-quarters full of water, then start shaking the pill dust into it. I swirl the liquid around and watch as some of the pill crystals absorb into the water, and the rest fall to the bottom of the cup. I move the cup toward Mr. Sands's mouth and put it up to his lips, pushing aside the vent tube in his mouth. I tilt the cup back, half expecting his eyes to snap open as the liquid drains down his throat. But this doesn't happen. Though something equally unexpected does: The solution starts dribbling down his chin and onto his hospital gown.

"Shit!" I say too loudly.

What if someone walks in here right now? He'll have a big wet spot on the front of his gown, and I'll be holding a plastic cup of liquid death.

My actions will kill him.

What I'm doing is illegal. I know this. I don't realize my hands are shaking, though, until I see the solution splashing around in the cup. I feel my stomach turn sour and I get that familiar, disturbing metallic taste in my mouth. *Don't throw up, don't throw up!* I'm beginning to lose my nerve, and then I hear footsteps coming down the hallway. I quickly put the cup back to his mouth to pour more in, but this time I lift his head off the pillow, letting it fall back against my hand in a gesture I hope will better open his throat. Most of the water goes down this time, but even after I pour down the contents, I know I have to do it all again.

Tears make everything blurry. More blurry. *What am I doing?*

I put the plastic cup down on the rolling cart where the pitcher sits and use the back of my other sleeve to wipe my face. I look at Mr. Sands lying there and then I glance at the photo of him, Isabelle, and their daughters that sits on the stand next to the bed. "This is what he wants," I whisper, as much to myself as to them. Then I turn away from the picture so I don't have to see Isabelle's face.

The voice of a woman in the hall comes closer and I can hear part of a conversation. It keeps getting louder and clearer. I duck down by the side of the bed, taking the rest of the pill dust and placing it at the bottom of the cup. Then I reach up to get the pitcher and pour in the water, again swirling it around to make sure as much of it dissolves as possible. I wait until the voice recedes. Whoever it was was probably just chatting on the phone, heading for the exit. But I wait another thirty seconds just to be safe. Before giving the cup to Mr. Sands, I search his face for a reason to stop. "Mr. Sands," I whisper. "Mr. Sands." I take his hand. "Oh my god," I exhale and blink away more tears. "You're supposed to be the one who stays." My tears catch in my voice. I give his hand a squeeze, then set it back down on the bed, and as I do, the voice in the hallway returns.

"Yeah, I'm comin', I'm comin'," the voice says to someone at the other end of the hallway. "Just need to check vitals in rooms three twenty and three twenty-two."

I have the sick certain feeling that woman will be walking into this room at any moment: My stomach drops to my knees and I know I have to get out of here. But first, I have to finish what I came here to do.

I take the cup and bring it to Mr. Sands's lips and pour the remaining solution down his throat. Then I take the sleeve of my shirt and rub it against his mouth, drying off his face and chest as best as I can.

I can't say it. I don't want to say good-bye. So I just turn away from him, grab my book bag, and rush for the door. I look left then right to make sure the nurse is still in the other room before I move. When I'm convinced it's all clear, I run down the hallway for the side door and slip out of the building. As soon as I'm outside, I pick up my bike, jump on it, and start sprinting. I pedal until the cramps in my calves force me to stop. And then I crumple at the waist, my elbows giving out and my chest dropping to the handlebars. I gasp for breath. As the cramps in my legs stop throbbing, the full force of what I've done slams into me and registers throughout my entire body: He's dying right now because of me.

I get off my bike and walk it the rest of the way home. When I finally get back to the house I unlock the door, numbly walk up the stairs, and collapse on my bed. I close my eyes but instead of darkness, I can only see Mr. Sands drifting out of consciousness.

Chapter Fourteen

When the alarm goes off the next morning, it feels like I've been asleep for less than a minute. I drag myself into the shower and then make the water as hot as possible. I try to feel something other than numb. I lift my chin in the direction of the showerhead, letting the steaming water beat down on my face. I don't know how long I stand there, but the only thing that makes me move is the banging on the bathroom door, and a shout informing me I need to vacate the premises. I towel off and keep my eyes down as I exit the bathroom, not yet ready to face Lolly or Mom. Not yet ready to face the day.

I dress quickly, go downstairs, and pour out a bowl of cereal, then stare into the bowl and start holding down the Corn Pops in the milk with my spoon. They resurface one by one.

What have I done?

What if it didn't work?

What if it did?

A wave of nausea hits me. I dump the rest of my cereal in the sink and wash the bowl as the next horrible thought hits me.

Isabelle.

I have to get out of here. I don't know where to go, but I need to outpace the thoughts in my head. Big Blue lies in the yard where I left it last night, but I don't think I'm steady enough to ride the bike this morning. Instead, I just start walking. I don't usually chew gum before 9:00 a.m., but I'd probably grind my teeth or gnaw through my cheek without it right now, so I put my hand in the side pocket of my bag to hunt for my pack.

As I slide my hand deeper into the pocket, I feel the blood drain from my face; the envelope containing my report card isn't in there. The envelope in which I'd kept Mr. Sands's pills. The envelope—with my name printed in full and no doubt some of the remaining semi-crushed pills that I'd used to "help" my friend—is missing.

"Wait, stop," I say aloud as if to reassure myself. I just must have missed it—it must be here. I stop dead in my tracks to look in the pocket, then burrow both hands deeper into the bag.

But it's not.

The envelope is not there.

I begin searching the main compartment more spas- tically now. The envelope isn't in there either. Okay, it must be here. It's gotta be here. I turn the bag inside out, dumping all the contents onto the ground—books, pens, papers, the mini-sock change purse where I keep all my cash, the small jug of gourmet syrup that I didn't even have time to give Mr. Sands.

Holy. Shit. It's not there. I must have left it in his room last night.

I scoop up everything from the ground and throw it back in my bag, starting to breathe very heavily as I jog-walk farther away from my house. I'd been worried about facing Isabelle, but now I have a new worry: facing criminal charges.

I have to get over to Hanover House to find that envelope before anyone else does. Thankfully Patty's not at the front desk when I arrive, just some woman I know only by sight. She nods hello.

"I forgot a book here yesterday!" I say as nonchalantly as possible, which is not at all nonchalant. I am sweating. I walk down the hallway toward the constant care ward and nod at the nurses on duty. "Left a book." I head straight for the room of Mr. Sands. But, oh god. There are two orderlies near his door. I walk past the room, trying to steal a peek inside and since I don't see the feet poking underneath the blanket on his bed, I double-back to look in again.

Mr. Sands isn't there. The room is empty. I don't know what I was expecting, but it wasn't this. I guess I wasn't really expecting him to be gone because it doesn't seem real and it doesn't seem possible that he could just vanish. That this man, this life force, could just cease to exist in some form . . . and that I'm responsible for vanishing him.

192

"Excuse me," I say to the male orderly. "Was Mr. Sands taken for some tests or something?"

"Oh, you mean the guy who was in this room?" he asks.

I nod. "Uh-huh, Frank Sands?"

"Yeah, he passed."

"What?"

"He died," he says, as if I need the translation.

"When?" I ask, needing to know the precise details of what happened after I left.

He shrugs his shoulders. Then the female orderly, who's holding a trash can and wearing a pair of rubber gloves, nods. "You mean the guy in here? I heard he passed in his sleep," she says. "I overheard the nurses talking about it. They were pretty upset. His wife found him early this morning before they'd come to do their rounds."

"Oh, no." I clasp my hand to my mouth. Hearing this description of the inevitable adds a whole new reality: He'll never smile again. Never crack a joke again. He'll never be able to say good-bye to his family. He's just gone. And it's because I helped him leave.

The man puts his hand on my shoulder. "He's in a better place," he tells me. As if *this* piece of information will calm me. "You know, he went quiet, in his sleep, like everyone wants to go."

"Do they know . . . do they know what caused it?" I ask.

"I don't know," he says, looking over to the woman, but she shakes her head.

"I think he was real sick, so . . ." she says.

I drift into the room, still hoping that Mr. Sands will be there, that there will be some trace of him. The two orderlies follow me. But Mr. Sands really isn't here. And neither is the envelope. "Where did they take him?" I ask.

"Funeral home came around this morning," the woman says. "I think they keep that place on speed dial over here." She cracks a smile and the man laughs, covering his mouth.

"You looking for something?" he then asks, noticing that I'm *not so nonchalantly* scanning the room.

How am I supposed to respond? Is it really smart or fantastically stupid to ask if they'd found an envelope of crushed-up pill dust in the room of a dead man? It's a question Eric could help me with, but that would mean confessing—and possibly making him an accessory to the crime. *If* it's a crime. And maybe it's not even, *maybe* it's euthanasia. But is that considered better or worse than assisted suicide? Or are they the same thing?

I'd been so sure that I'd never be suspected that it never occurred to me that I could be caught! Suddenly all of the legal questions I should have asked myself before I made the decision to help Mr. Sands—all of the things that would have been important to think about when I was focused on stopping his suffering—now attack my brain.

"Um, well actually I can't find the envelope with my

report card in it, and I thought I might have left it there when I was in his room yesterday." I nod.

"And you probably need to get that signed by your mom, right?" the woman asks, now with a note of sympathy in her voice. "Well, when someone passes, they try to get the room cleared as quick as possible so it don't upset the other residents. Night crew might still have been on duty, so you should ask Miro, the head of sanitation."

What I should do is get out of here before my head explodes. "Okay, thanks," I say. I need to see Isabelle, but I can't bring myself to do it.

Not now.

Not yet.

But as I leave Hanover House and head to school, I take out my phone and start dialing her number. I'm not sure what I'm going to say, not even sure that I won't hang up as soon as she answers.

"Hello?" says a female voice I don't recognize.

"Is Isabelle there?"

"She's resting now," the voice replies curtly.

"Well, do you know when she might be up?"

"No, she's been given some medication to help her sleep. She's had a very difficult morning."

"Yeah," I say, "I know."

"Would you like to leave a message?"

I have to think about this for a moment. "Yes, please. Thank you. Could you just tell her that Grace called and I'm sorry about . . ." My voice catches and I can't finish the sentence.

"Of course, dear," the voice says, softening. "It's very nice of you to call."

The image of Mr. and Mrs. Sands in that wedding photo floats through my mind—that, combined with the idea that I'm responsible for taking Isabelle's husband away from her . . .

I spend the entire day at school in a fog. Nothing registers and nothing seems quite real. I don't speak a word to anyone. I have two classes with Eric today, but I'm careful to avoid his glance and I skip lunch, spending the period in the girls' room instead. Hidden in a stall, I examine my hands, the knuckles, the fingers, the palms: the hands that did the deed. When I look up, I don't bother asking if what I did was right or wrong. It's too late for that one now. I simply ask *What next?*

No response.

When the school day ends, I can't stay away. I have to see Isabelle. I'm scheduled to work at Hanover House this afternoon, but I don't bother checking in at the Activities Office; instead I head straight back to the Sandses' cottage. The screen door is open behind the screen, so I knock, then enter.

"Hello?" I say, not seeing her. "Isabelle?" I move through the house, as if on a mission. And then I see her. She's in her bedroom, lying flat out over the white eyelet bedspread, her arms folded over her chest, and for a moment, I'm convinced she's dead too. She decided living life without her husband wasn't worth it. She couldn't go on. Her heart literally broke. And it was my fault.

My heart catches in my chest and I gasp. Isabelle's eyes open and she looks at me hovering. "Grace," she says, her lips turned down, her wide-set brown eyes rimmed with red. "You heard about Frank?"

I nod.

"He passed away peacefully in his sleep this morning." She sits up, rubs her eyes, then reaches out for me to take her hand. "That's what he said he always wanted. 'Izzy, I just want to fall asleep and not wake up,' he'd say. 'You may not get to cheat death, but at least you get to cheat the alarm clock!'" She laughs a little at this. "That was my Frank."

When she says this, I hear myself exhale. "Well, I'm glad he went the way he wanted."

Isabelle shakes her head. "This is what he wanted, but it's not what I wanted. It's all my fault."

"That's not true," I say quickly, but she doesn't react. We sit there for another moment and I stare at my hand in hers. The hand that turned her life upside down.

"Oh, Grace, what am I going to do now?" Isabelle asks, fresh tears springing to her eyes.

"Um." I shake my head, incapable of saying anything more helpful or profound because of the plum-sized lump rising in my throat. I need to tell her what I did, but I now feel so guilty about what my actions have done to *her*, I can't get it out. I feel like I'm suffocating.

"That's okay." She rubs my hand and smiles a bit. "I don't have any idea either. But I'm sure my daughters will have some opinions on the subject." Isabelle rolls her eyes, then looks skyward. "Sarah will be back here shortly and Jill, my younger daughter, is making her way back from Paris and should be in over the weekend."

"Well," I say, drawing back a sob, "that should be nice, to be surrounded by family."

"Just between us," Isabelle replies, lowering her voice, "I'm sort of dreading it."

"You are?"

"It's just that it will make all of this very real. Very final, you know?" Isabelle closes her eyes and exhales. After a few moments of silence, she looks back to me. "I just keep expecting Frank to walk through the front door like he used to do, day in and day out. Isn't that ridiculous?"

"No, it's not." I shake my head. "But maybe that's why it'll be good to have your daughters with you."

Isabelle takes a moment, then she stands up and smoothes down her skirt. "I'm sorry, Grace, can I get you something to drink?"

"Oh, uh, I don't want to put you to any trouble."

"I think I'm going to have a little whiskey, myself," she says. "I know it's not yet five p.m., but I don't really care." Isabelle walks to the kitchen and I follow behind her.

She takes the bottle of Jack Daniels from the cabinet and then takes down two glass tumblers. She starts pouring the dark orangey-gold liquid into one of the glasses and fills it halfway. "Would you like some?"

"I'm not really sure if I should."

"Well, of course you shouldn't, but that's not what I asked you," Isabelle says. "You do want some, don't you?"

I can tell she wants me to have this drink with her. I've tried alcohol before, but I never really liked it. I don't want her to have to have this drink alone, though, so I nod.

"Yeah, okay, thanks," I say, taking the glass that she's already poured for me. I wait until she pours one for herself to lift it up to my lips.

"To better days," Isabelle toasts, taking a swallow.

The smell penetrates my nose before the stinging liquid hits my tongue and starts burning down my esophagus. I cough a little. I didn't expect the drink to be nearly as powerful as it is. It's what I imagine lighter fluid would taste like. "Strong," I say.

This makes Isabelle laugh. "Strong indeed." She smiles. "You do get used to it, but it always remains blessedly strong."

"Does it ever start tasting better?" I hesitantly put my nose back toward the cup.

"Just tastes strong to me," she says. "And especially at times like these, I think that tastes good. Come on, let's get some cheese and crackers and sit in the living room like ladies, shall we?" She moves toward the refrigerator, but when her hands land on a wedge of white cheese flecked with blue veins, an idea comes to me.

"Actually, why don't I make us a little something?" I say, taking a few items out of the refrigerator.

"Sure, whatever you like." Isabelle leans against the counter and swirls the drink in her hand, looking into the depths of her glass as if it contained an answer.

I find the rest of the things I need and grab a mixing bowl from beneath the sink. I don't bother looking for the measuring cups. I just estimate the ingredients as I add them together and start beating the mixture until I have the right consistency: smooth but for some character lumps.

"Do you have a griddle?"

Isabelle shakes her head and takes a swallow of her drink with a look that seems to convey terrible disappointment. "That's okay, really, it's no problem," I reply, taking another quick swig from my cup and opening the cabinet under the range to find a frying pan. When I see one that's suitably large, I turn the burner to medium, then toss in a pat of butter to grease the pan. As it heats, the butter skates around the pan's surface, leaving behind a wet, whitish trail as it melts into oblivion. I lift up the handle and roll my wrist, speeding its fade.

I find a ladle in the utensil drawer and spoon out the batter into four good-sized dollops, then sneak a look back at Isabelle, who's standing there, staring blankly out the window. I glance out to see what she's looking at, but there's nothing there; she just looks inconsolably lonely. I take another sip of my drink, then turn my attention back to the pancakes and wait for the bubbles to appear. When Isabelle lets out a sigh behind me, it gives me the chills and I get the strangest feeling that the bubbles won't rise to the surface today. It almost seems like the atmosphere here's too heavy to support them, as if their lightness would be offensive.

But then all of a sudden and out of nowhere, one bubbles up.

And then another.

And then four more bubbles cluster at the edge of one of the pancakes. As each bursts into the world, unaffected by anything that's come before or will happen after, the bubbles take their privileged moments in time. I know what needs to be done now, so spatula in hand, I flip the pancakes before they burn. Isabelle looks over to me when she hears the spatula scrape the pan.

"Pancakes?" she asks.

"Comfort food," I reply. "There's just something about pancakes that makes me feel better."

"Then I'm glad you made them." She raises her glass to me. "But I'm sorry, I don't think we have any syrup."

The small jug of syrup is sitting in my bag, but there's no way in hell I can take it out now. "Really not a big deal," I answer. "We don't need it." When they're ready I turn off the burner and plate the pancakes. "Here you go, Isabelle," I say, handing her two good-looking flapjacks.

"Thank you, Grace, and my true friends call me Izzy, so you should, too." She gathers the contents of our impromptu cocktail and pancake party and walks to the living room.

When we sit down, Isabelle leans back into the couch and puts her feet up on the coffee table. "I don't know what I'm going to do when my daughters get here," she says, taking a forkful of pancake and closing her eyes. "Mmm, that is good, thank you."

"What do you mean you don't know what you'll do?" I ask, lifting my fork and taking a bite. It's good, but it really *could* use a little syrup . . .

Isabelle takes another swallow of her drink and puckers her lips. "My daughters don't really like me."

"That can't be true."

"No, it is. I know it's true. There was never one big falling out, and yet, there's just this *thing* between us. This ugly gray cloud that just hangs there. I don't know where I went wrong with them," she says with a shake of her head. She looks down into her glass and swirls the liquid before taking a sip.

"Well, did you ever think it's them—their fault—not yours?" I drink more, hoping to show I'm totally on her side. I want to do anything I can to make her feel better right now. "I mean, make them step up."

"It's hard for a mother to do that, Grace. I'm the one who raised them after all, so somehow it all has to be my fault, doesn't it?"

"No," I reply. "Un-uh." Do I blame my mother for the relationship we have? . . . Okay, maybe that's a bad example.

Isabelle pauses, then takes another generous swallow of her whiskey. "Still, I always hoped—I'd always assumed—that things would eventually even out. That we'd all be okay with one another at some point. Now, with Frank's death, I can't even imagine what they'll think of me." She raises her eyebrows and the lines on her forehead run together.

I rack my brain for something smart to say, but it's not like I've got any wisdom to offer, and I don't exactly have any insight from the relationship I have with my mother to give. So I just force down a big gulp of my drink, then slice off a hunk of the pancake. But before I put the fork to my mouth, I dunk it in the whiskey. Not bad.

"Now there's some ingenuity," she replies with a smile, pouring more Jack Daniels into both of our glasses and then dunking a forkful of pancake into hers. "Yeah, that's nice. And you know what? I think it *is* making me feel better," she says. "You know I can't recall when I had my first drink—I suppose I was about your age in high school—but it's amazing how quickly the time goes. I remember when I was younger, summer seemed to last forever. And a school year just went on and on."

"No kidding," I say, "and it's so weird because weekends will pass in the blink of an eye, but the school week drags like the rusty tailpipe off the back of a Chevy Impala."

"I think that whiskey's making a poet out of you, Grace." She laughs. "But you're right, we're taught to think of time as a constant, measured off in minutes, hours, and days. But it sure doesn't feel that way." She takes another sizable swallow, and I, still following her lead, do the same. The warm feeling in my stomach is beginning to spread to my arms and legs and it feels good.

I wonder what my mother would have to say about this conversation if she were here. Until this talk with Izzy, I'd never thought things wouldn't get better with my mother either. I know we're at each other a lot and have all sorts of stupid fights, but I guess I just didn't think that would really continue. Or maybe it's more that I never really bothered thinking about us in the future.

"Mom," a voice calls out, before the sound of a rapid knocking at the screen door.

"Speak of the devil," Isabelle says softly, standing up. "Come on in, Sarah, I'm in the living room."

"I should go, Izzy," I say, liking the way her nickname sounds coming out of my mouth.

"No, please, Grace," she replies, taking hold of my hand again. I'm a little startled by the gesture, and when I hesitate briefly she says, "I mean, only stay if you want to, but I'd like it if you did."

There is no way I'm going to say no to this woman. So when the door opens and Sarah, the woman I'd seen before with Izzy in Mr. Sands's room, walks in, I just stand there and wait for Izzy to explain me.

"Hi?" Sarah says, nodding at me with a half smile as she walks over to Isabelle and gives her a hug.

"Sarah, this is Grace. I've asked her to stay with me for a little while," Izzy replies to the unasked "Who is this kid and when is she leaving?" question.

"I'm so sorry about your father," I say, my head shaking back and forth. I really want—*need*—Sarah to know how much Mr. Sands meant to me. "He was so great. I liked him so much."

But these words don't seem enough. They can't even touch the relationship we had. They don't convey the strength of his presence in my life, and the fact that one of the things I liked most was that the steadiness didn't mean seriousness. Mr. Sands taught me that despite whatever drama was playing out, it was not only okay but *important* to find the humor in the situation, dark though it might be. And he reminded me to laugh because that's what gives life color.

"I gave him a Mohawk," I add, nodding at Sarah.

"Oh, uh-huh," she replies, turning away from me.

But Isabelle laughs, getting it. "And Dad sure liked her," she says, smiling at me, then looking back to Sarah.

"Cole's right behind me." Sarah angles her head toward the door. "He's just parking the car."

"Oh, wonderful. Well, Grace and I were just having a little afternoon snack. Can I offer you something to drink?" Izzy asks, almost formally.

Sarah takes a look at the remnants of our snack. "Mom, is that whiskey?" She eyes my glass and looks at me.

"It is," Izzy answers in a tone so blasé, it almost sounds like a reprimand. "Would you like a bit? It'll warm you right up."

"No," Sarah says, moving quickly to clear our tumblers and dumping them in the kitchen sink. Izzy raises her eyebrows at me and I shrug. Well, I really didn't want any more to drink anyway since I'm feeling a little wobbly, but that was *kind of* rude.

The door opens a moment later and I first see the silhouette of a muscular guy who's probably six feet tall. When I first see the shadow I imagine it's Mr. Sands in his younger days, coming through the door, back from work, just like Isabelle mentioned. But as the figure enters the room and walks toward Isabelle, I see that he's got dark floppy hair, big brown eyes, and is probably a year or so older than me. That must be the little kid from the picture! Boy, time does move quickly.

"Hi Grandma," he says to Isabelle as he moves next to Sarah.

"Cole, come here and give me a hug," Isabelle replies. Cole glances at his mother, who lifts her head as if to say "go." As Cole walks toward Isabelle, she turns to me and says, "If he thinks he's going to get away without giving his grandmother a hug, he's got another thing coming!"

There's some awkward laughter during the uncomfortable embrace, and when Isabelle finally releases Cole, who immediately walks back over to his mom's side, she says, "Grace, this is my handsome grandson, Cole."

"Hello, Handsome," I reply, before I realize *that* isn't his name. . . . "I mean Cole! Cole, hi." A blush fire of mortification burns through my cheeks.

"Hey," he says with a laugh and a slight blush himself.

"Grace works here at Hanover House as a doctor or a candy striper, I can't remember which," she says with a laugh.

Even though I *might* be a little bit tipsy, I can see

Sarah staring at her mother, wondering if she's drunk. I'm actually beginning to wonder the same thing myself. But drunk or not, Isabelle does seem a little happier now than when I first came in, and if that's the effect of the alcohol, I'd gladly pour her another drink.

"Mom," Sarah says in an authoritative voice, "I think we should go out and get you a dress now."

"I don't need a new dress, but thank you, Sarah, that's very nice of you to offer," she replies.

"No, Mom," Sarah says, with an exhale implying she doesn't want to be doing this either. "I mean a dress for the funeral on Wednesday."

It's not as if Isabelle hadn't been thinking of the upcoming funeral, but I think she had momentarily managed to put it out of her mind, so when Sarah says this, it's as if a cloud of sadness drops back over Izzy's face.

"Oh, right," she replies, sitting back down on the couch. "Well, whatever you think is best."

"I think we should go and do it now," Sarah says. "If you'll excuse us, Grace, we'll need to leave to get to the stores before they close."

I shoot Izzy a look, checking in to see if it's okay for me to leave, but she's staring at the floor now and seems to have retreated into her own thoughts. "Well, I should probably get back to the main house," I say. "I'll see you later, Iz—Mrs. Sands."

"Good-bye Grace," she replies as she escorts me to

the door, "and thank you for the pancakes and the company." She takes my hand between hers and I can feel something press between us. "Promise me you'll use it on something that will give you a little happiness, okay? Because I know that would make Frank happy, and that would mean a lot to me."

When I get outside, I look in my hand and I see it's a fifty-dollar bill that she's folded in fourths. Her kindness only makes me feel worse about what I've done, so I need to get rid of this money as quickly as I can. I go to the one place that's reliably given me comfort when I've been upset before, Milk Bar.

As I walk to the coffee shop, I think about what I'll order: a hot chocolate with whipped cream, and a peanut butter chip chocolate muffin. If that doesn't make me feel better, at least it should send me into some form of sugar shock. I notice a Help Wanted sign taped up to the bottom of the coffee shop's window and wonder what it'd be like to work here, how the only decision you'd be forced to make is deciding which customers deserve the bigger muffins, and which deserve the runts. I think about how different my life would be if I'd just picked a harmless job like this. But before I place my order, I glance over to the tables and get another surprise. Sitting one table over from where we last sat are Eric and Natalie. She's laughing at something he just said or did and he looks down grinning, clearly pleased by her reaction. But when Eric looks up, our eyes connect and he gives me a different type of smile. It seems to be one that says "You caught me."

"Grace," Eric says. "Hey."

"Hey," I reply, trying to decide if I have to go over to talk to them.

"Oh, hi, Grace!" Natalie replies. "Come join us."

There is no way in hell I am going to *come on over and join* them. "Yeah, thanks, but I can't." Eric and I haven't really spoken since our last encounter about Natalie, and now isn't exactly the optimal time. "I just came to pick up a job application." I point to the Help Wanted sign in the window as proof of my lie.

"Did you quit Hanover House?" Natalie asks. "I mean, I would've. I don't know how you've lasted this long. It's so depressing over there."

"You quit Hanover House?" Eric repeats.

"No. Not yet." I shake my head, which wobbles back and forth a bit thanks to the whiskey. "Just wanted to check out my options, see what else is out there. I'm sure you know how it is."

Eric doesn't respond to this, but Natalie does. "Yeah, I think it's really important to do that. I mean, how else are you going to know what you like and don't like?"

"Right, well, I should get going," I say. "See ya."

"Grace," Eric calls out as I turn, "call me later, okay?"

I nod—wanting to scream—and then grab the

employment application form from the counter and stick it in the back pocket of my jeans before leaving. Unfortunately I'm still holding the money Isabelle gave me there too, and I need to lose it as quickly as possible . . .

The mall isn't close, and it's at the end of a dangerous stretch of road, but I don't care. I start walking there aggressively as if daring the cars to mess with me now. When I finally arrive, I walk right past the store where I'd last come with Eric, and I don't go into the chain stores where I normally shop. Instead I head for Cignal. It's a store where the more stylish girls at school buy their clothes, and I know this thanks to the T-shirts they wear with *Cignal* printed boldly across their chests.

I've never been inside the store before—it always seemed like one of those places where anyone not in the in-crowd isn't welcome. So as I pass through the alarm detectors on both sides of the doorway, I get a little jittery. I'm even intimidated by the mannequins. In fairness, these are no friendly mannequins; they're the kind that don't wear wigs. Like they're too cool to be burdened by hair, and their cheekbones are so sharp, they look like they could cut you. The salesgirls don't look much friendlier. In fact, they're practically all as angular as their plastic counterparts and I can feel them staring at me, sizing me up, wondering what I'm doing here.

One of the live girls, a saleslady who looks like she's probably in her mid-twenties, approaches. "Were you looking for anything special today?" she asks, then smiles, holding it until I respond.

I don't really want to explain, but I suddenly want to get a rise out of her. "I need a dress I can wear to a friend's funeral."

"Oh," she replies, instantly dropping the fake smile. "Well, I'm not sure we're going to have a huge selection for that, but we do have a lot of stuff in black?" She says this as if it's a question, but really it's the perfect response.

"Um, yeah, sure."

The woman leads me over to a rack of dresses toward the back. "What do you think about this?" she asks, pulling out a simple black number with a keyhole cut-out down the front of the chest.

"I don't know."

"Maybe this?" She presents a black-and-white houndstooth print that looks like something a stylish "career gal" might wear.

"Not really my style," I reply, as if I have some sort of defined "funeral style" that I wear to all the best burials.

Then I see it: the perfect dress. The material looks like brushed satin and it seems like something Audrey Hepburn would have worn in *Breakfast at Tiffany's*. It's a sleeveless top that gathers tightly at the waist, then poufs out like a bell in the skirt. The best part is the color: It's a brilliant, deep red. The saleslady sees me eyeing it and starts shaking her head.

"You know," she says, "that dress doesn't really scream 'funeral' to me."

"Yeah, that's kind of what I like about it." Of course I have no intention of buying a new dress to wear to Mr. Sands's funeral. But there's something about this dress that calls to me. "I'm going to try it on," I say. "Where's the dressing room?"

She points me in the direction of a curtained-off area and even as I hold the dress in my hand I can already picture myself in it—or how I want to look in it, anyway. I slip off my shoes and yank down my jeans, then carefully unzip the delicate zipper at the back of the dress. The fabric feels cool against my skin when I put it on, and I contort my arms so I can close the zipper without having to ask the woman for help. I'm almost afraid to look in the mirror, but when I finally get up the nerve to take my eyes off my feet, I'm stunned at what I see. The dress, narrower at the top and flaring gently wider toward the bottom, looks good—looks like it was made for me, in fact—and flatters my figure in a way that I didn't even know was possible. I walk out of the dressing room and the salesgirl's face registers surprise.

"Wow," she says, "that looks great on you, but—"

"But what?" I wonder if actually makes my butt

look huge or if my back fat is somehow bulging out in unsightly lumps.

"But I'm just not sure you can wear it to a funeral," she says seriously. "I mean, look, we work on commission, so I should probably just keep my mouth shut or try to convince you to buy this, but I think I might feel a little guilty if I did."

Unbelievable. Who knew I'd find the one salesgirl in this obnoxious store with a strong code of ethics? And because she's being honest, I feel a little bad about continuing the lie too.

"Well, red was his favorite color, so this is sort of like a tribute." I nod. (Okay, so it turns out I don't really feel bad at all about continuing the lie.)

"Oh." She nods back. "Then you should get it, because that A-line really does look fabulous on you."

"Thanks," I say brightly. "I'm going to take it." I walk back into the dressing room and unzip the dress, putting it on the hanger before even bothering to look at the price tag. Steeling myself for sticker shock, I'm still stunned when I see the printed price, $480. But there's a red slash through it and a blue circle sticker on top, so I call out to the saleslady on the other side of the curtain.

"Excuse me?"

"Yes?" she replies, sounding uncomfortably close to the curtain.

"There's a red slash through the price on this dress,

so I was wondering if you could tell me how much it is now." I hand the dress over the top of the curtain and she takes it from me.

I can hear her let out a little laugh. "Today must be your lucky day," she says, before instantly retracting it with a, "Um, I didn't exactly mean . . . Well, anyway, I think this dress must have been around for a little while—maybe it was here waiting for you!—because it was marked down by fifty percent, then twenty-five percent off that."

I do the math as quickly as I can and even though $180 was still way more money than I wanted to spend on a dress I wasn't planning to buy, I can't *not* buy it now. But I do manage to restrain myself from saying *I'll be the luckiest girl at the funeral!*

I find my change purse at the bottom of my bag and count the cash I've stashed inside. Between the money I've been saving from my job and what Isabelle had given me every now and again, I have just enough to cover it. I watch with no small amount of pride as the saleslady carefully folds the dress before laying it out on a cocoon of tissue paper. She takes a satisfying amount of time creasing the tissue paper to make sure the dress won't wrinkle before she puts the store's sticker against it, wrapping it up like the present that it is. She then takes one of the large Cignal shopping bags and flutters it open with a proper flourish, and slides the dress inside before handing it over to me.

"You're going to look great," she says with a smile. "I'm sure your friend would be really pleased if he could see you."

"Thanks." I awkwardly smile back at her, thinking about Mr. Sands and knowing she's probably right.

Chapter Fifteen

School blurs the next day, and I head over to Hanover House as soon as the bell rings. It's not a work day, I just don't know where else I should be. When I enter the cottage, Izzy's holding a plate of large, moist-looking cookies. "Oatmeal raisin?" she offers, pointing me to the couch. "Esther Newman just dropped them off, so they're probably pretty good. That woman doesn't have much on the ball, but she is a great cook, which I suppose should count for something." Isabelle lowers her voice. "Oh, and you should see the ugly dress Sarah insisted I buy yesterday. It's awful."

"Maybe it isn't as bad as you think," I reply, reaching for a cookie and biting into it. "This *is* good, you should have one."

Isabelle takes a medium-sized cookie for herself and takes a bite. "No, that dress is beyond ugly. But that's what I wanted because I have every intention of burning it after I wear it on Wednesday. I have no plans to keep a memento of my husband's funeral sitting around in my closet. That's why I purposefully got the cheapest dress I could find so I wouldn't feel bad about spending Sarah's money, then throwing it away. Let people talk if they want to."

"You think people would talk about your dress?" I ask.

"People talk about everything here. No topic too small to dissect," Isabelle replies.

"Well, I'd try to keep those folks away from the funeral if you can. Seems like the one time you really shouldn't have to deal with people you don't want to."

"You're right." Isabelle hands me a cup of tea. "But part of what makes them so miserable is that they can't take the hint. Do you know when Esther came up to me that first night after Frank . . . well, she took my hand and said, 'Isabelle, I know just exactly how you feel!' And do you know all I wanted to do was knock that horrible woman to the ground? She had *no idea* how I was feeling. How could she?" Isabelle shakes her head. "She didn't know the relationship that I had with Frank. She had no idea what we'd been through together."

Again, I think about telling her what I did; confessing the truth. I wanted to do right by Mr. Sands, and I want to do right by Isabelle too, but I don't know if hearing this would make her feel better or worse. And the last thing I want to do is make her suffer more now . . . I already feel guilty enough for the pain I've caused her.

The doorbell rings. "Ah," Isabelle says, "must be some of my friends. They told me they'd be coming over shortly." She nods. "That is one of the nice things about being in a place like this. You have a big community of people who are there for you." She sighs. "Sometimes I hate the closeness—it's like you can't escape people, almost like high school—but sometimes there is comfort in it. Grace, would you be good enough to get that? I'm going to go to the powder room to freshen up for a minute."

"No problem." When I open the door, two women I've seen around the grounds are standing there. "Hi, I'm Grace. I'm a candy striper," I say, feeling like I should somehow justify my presence here.

"Oh, that's right. I'm Mrs. Thompson and this is Mrs. Savitz." Mrs. Thompson is a few inches smaller than me, as is Mrs. Savitz, and they both have the old-lady helmet hairdo that is flattering on no one. I guess when you hit a certain age, you don't want to waste time blow-drying, so you cut it short. But it's kind of funny that as a result, everyone winds up with the same 'do as if it's a standard issue uniform, again, not unlike a trend in high school.

Mrs. Savitz is holding a plate of something covered in tinfoil. "Is she resting?" she asks.

"No, she's just in the bathroom. She'll be right out," I say.

"Okay." Mrs. Thompson nods. "Well, we're here now, so you can go."

"Oh. Right." I didn't realize that their arrival necessarily meant my departure, and I don't particularly want to leave. "Well, I'll just wait to say good-bye to her until she comes out."

Mrs. Savitz smiles at me as the two women come in and sit on the couch. "Do you know what the plans are for the funeral, Grace?"

"I know it's supposed to be Wednesday in the late afternoon," I say. "I think they're waiting for her younger daughter to make it in from overseas."

"Well, that should give them enough time to do the autopsy," Mrs. Thompson clucks.

Autopsy?

"I didn't know they were planning to do an autopsy," I reply as coolly as I can.

"I don't think they were," she responds, "but I'm going to convince Izzy that she needs to have one. With all the questionable medical treatment people get here, it's a wonder if they didn't outright kill Frank, the poor man."

My heart starts racing. If they do an autopsy, they're sure to find evidence of the pills I gave Mr. Sands. And then they'd be forced to launch an investigation . . . and then the missing report card envelope with trace evidence, which, once I'd heard funeral plans were set, I stopped obsessing over, would come back to haunt me . . . Sweat begins to bead on my upper lip.

"Hello Ronnie, hello Shirley," Isabelle says when she reenters the room, "so nice of you to come."

"I'm going to go," I say to Isabelle quickly.

"Well okay, Grace, thank you again for stopping by."

"Uh-huh." I nod, mopping my forehead with my hand and walking to the door.

"Grace, wait," Isabelle says, and I see her scanning the room for her purse.

"No." I shake my head at her, silently trying to convey that I desperately don't want to take any of her money.

But she either doesn't understand my signal or is choosing to ignore it. I see her discreetly take a bill from her wallet and crush it in her palm as she walks over to me by the door. "And if not before, can I expect to see you Wednesday afternoon?" she asks, pressing the cash in my hand, without saying the words "at the funeral."

"I'll be there," I respond, now wondering if that funeral could also be my own.

♪♪ ♪♪ ♪♪

I stare at the ceiling in my room and think about the time I broke my wrist. I'd never realized how important my wrist was until suddenly I couldn't use it anymore. I broke it when I tripped in my flip-flops. I'd put out my arm to break the fall and wound up breaking the wrist in two places instead. I wore a fiberglass cast for eight weeks and it was only during that time that I realized how much I'd relied on that wrist and how I'd always just taken it for granted before. When the cast finally came off, the wrist was much scrawnier than my other one since the surrounding muscles had atrophied. But getting that wrist back was like a gift, and for the first few days, I stared at it like it hadn't been a part of my body for my whole life.

My father's presence was also something I took for granted. Until he left. And in Dad's absence was Mr. Sands, who didn't replace him but helped fill the hole. Now that he's gone, too, I'm just left feeling broken, and I could use help picking up the pieces.

Since no one else seems to be answering my messages, I think, staring at the blank ceiling above, I wonder if it's time to call my father back and tell him he's needed? That I need him. But before I can bring myself to make the call, I lock myself in the bathroom and rehearse what I'm going to say in the mirror. I try to imagine what his face will look like after I've said my piece. My hands shake as I hold the cell phone, but thankfully I have him on speed dial so I won't have to worry about hitting the right keys. Still, even pushing the TALK button takes concentration. On the first ring I remind myself to act cool. By the second, my index finger hovers over the END button. On the third ring he picks up.

"Hullo?"

"Dad, hey, it's me. Grace." I stare at my face in the mirror and wonder if I would look different to him now, if I've changed at all in the months he's been gone, or in the events of the past few weeks.

"Grace! Hey! Wow, great to hear from you. I've been trying to get in touch with you, you know. Left a lot of messages on your cell phone."

"Oh, yeah, I guess I never got them." Hadn't planned to start out with a lie, but I can't seem to help myself.

"Well, that's okay, I've got you now, right? So how are you? How have you been?"

"It's kind of been a tough year."

Dad pauses. I've caught him off guard, and in the momentary silence I can almost hear him wonder what the best response to my statement will be. "Oh, yeah?" he replies. "Your classes are hard, huh?"

He chose the wrong one. "I guess," I say.

"So how's your social life? Breaking a lot of hearts, I'll bet."

Breaking a lot of hearts? "Yeah, I guess you could say that," I reply, and Dad laughs too loudly. I'll give him another chance. "So, Dad, I was just wondering, think you'll be coming back home anytime soon?"

Dad stops laughing and I hear him exhale. "Well, that's a tough question, Gracie."

I want to tell him that he has *no idea* what a tough question is. I want to tell him that he's the adult, so he's supposed to have the answers. Instead I manage, "Yeah. Okay. So?"

"Well, there are a lot of factors. And your mother's probably pretty angry with me, which I can understand."

"Me too," I reply, hoping he'll catch both meanings of my response.

"But maybe I can take you and Lolly out to IHOP this

week? Whaddya say? I can't believe it's been almost a year since I've seen my girls. I miss you."

"I don't know, Dad." This conversation is not going at all in the way I wanted it to. Not that I even knew what that was supposed to be. "I might not be able to."

"Your mother can't stop me from seeing my daughters," he says, his voice swelling with righteous indignation.

"No, I just meant I've got some stuff that I'll be dealing with, and I'm not sure I'll be able to make it, that's all."

"Well, how much more important could the stuff be than seeing your dear old dad, huh? We haven't seen each other in months."

His words are like the final straw on the load. "It's not like you didn't know where to find us," I reply, pissed.

"Look, Grace, I am sorry you haven't gotten my calls, but I have been trying to get in touch," he offers. Insufficiently.

"Is your new life better, Dad?"

"You're angry."

"You think?" I reply, noticing the red flare in my cheeks in the mirror. "I'm not even sure why I called. I just thought, in case you started hearing things— maybe that I'd done something some people might consider bad—I wanted you to know I did it for the right reasons."

"Grace, I'm not really following you," Dad says.

"I know," I reply, "I'm probably not making much sense, but I just wanted you to know that I did what I did because I thought it was the right thing. And I'm not sorry about that."

"Honey," he says, his voice softening now, "that's how I always tried to raise you, to be a good Christian and to do the right thing . . . What did you do, Grace?"

"I gotta go, Dad."

"Well, can I call you again another time?" he asks.

"Yeah."

"And you'll actually pick up when you see it's me?"

He laughs.

"Probably."

"Thank you," he says, then, "You know I love you, right?"

"Okay, bye, Dad," I reply, and hit END.

♪ ♪ ♪

I toss and turn the whole night. My eyes burn open every few minutes, drawn to the bright green numbers on the clock, which seem to be mocking me. It's as if I'm being told I don't deserve sleep. Innocent people get to sleep, but this is how the guilty conscience is punished. *No sleep for the wicked,* isn't that how it goes? I try to bargain my way into it somehow: "Let me fall asleep now and I'll be good—I'll be a better student. I'll be nicer to my mother. I'll make sure Isabelle is always comfortable. I won't do anything wrong again."

No deal.

But why should I be surprised? Who am I even trying to bargain with? I've put in a lot of requests over the past few weeks and it's not like I've gotten any evidence that anyone's out there. Or listening. Or giving a damn. So what's the point?

When it's absolutely clear to me that regardless of how tired I am, I won't be able to sink into oblivion, I get out of bed. It's so early it's still dark outside, and for some reason it occurs to me that I should go for a run—*clearly I'm not in my right head*. But maybe it'll let me feel like I'm leaving my problems behind at least temporarily.

I put on a T-shirt, sweats, and since I don't have proper running shoes, I just lace up my Pumas extra tight before heading out the door. When I get to the end of the block, I realize I should have brought my music with me, but I'm not going to go back for it, because I'll probably just stop if I don't keep running.

So that's what I do: I keep up my pace and I keep moving, one foot in front of the other until I can hear myself breathing heavily. It doesn't take long before I get a stabbing pain in my left side, but I run through it. At least the pain is something for me to focus on outside my head.

I don't have a destination in mind, but when I see the hill at the far side of the community park, I know that's where I'll head. The grass in the park is still wet with dew and I kick up some of the water and mud against my calves. I can feel myself gaining speed as I take the hill, and though pain is radiating up my shins, I have no intention of slowing down. I push myself to get to the top and when I do, sweating, out of breath, and with pinpricks of pain shooting through my legs, I look across the horizon.

I stare at the orangey ball of sun that is now rising through the tree line in front of me. I bend over, dropping my hands to my knees without taking my eyes off the sight before me. I don't remember ever having been present at a sunrise before, and as I watch the fog start to burn off and the air clearing in front of me, it's hard not to be taken with the absolute beauty of a new day dawning. I've never really pondered the sunrise before. But standing here now, watching it happen, it's amazing and it's powerful, and it happens every single day with or without us. That's when it strikes me that if you have nothing else to believe in, there's always this. This is universal. This is something to be thankful for. Whatever else you accept as true—God or no God—this can't be denied, and it's the same for all of us, which means even in our darkest hours, we are all connected; we are not alone. I don't know if this is what having faith means, but I get the feeling that wherever Mr. Sands is, he remains with me, part of the dawn.

Chapter Sixteen

There's a quiet hum in the air Wednesday afternoon, like that slightly electrical feeling that remains in the atmosphere after a summer thunderstorm. I never understood the phrase "quiet after the storm," since things are never perfectly quiet really. Quiet by comparison, maybe, but there's always some splashing around, tree limbs falling, animals shaking off their coats. I think what people are really talking about is the sound of things settling. That's what I'm hearing inside my own head right now. And as I walk to the Bartel Funeral Home to attend the service of Frank Sands, I don't think I've ever heard such an eerie non-sound before.

The service is taking place in the home's main chapel, and I sit at the end of one of the pews a few rows from the back. I examine the packed crowd but barely recognize any of the faces. *Who are all these people?* Sure it's great that so many of them showed up, but why did so few visit Mr. Sands at Hanover House while he was still alive? I don't even know if I should be here. Yes, Isabelle asked me to come, but if I'd confessed and told her what I'd done—that I'm the one responsible for this day—I'm sure she'd hate the thought of me sitting in this room with her and her family.

Isabelle sits in the front row, flanked by her daughters. She's wearing large dark sunglasses that cover half her face, so it's impossible to tell what she's focusing on right now. I can't help but think that she's not just mourning the loss of her husband here. As the person left behind, she must also be mourning her own life. The life she knew died with him.

When the minister enters he nods to her, then walks to the podium by the casket, which is draped with a large arrangement of flowers. I can practically hear Mr. Sands complaining about them. "Look at all those damn flowers, Grace!" he'd say. "What are they trying to do, make me look like I won the Kentucky Derby? If they really wanted me to rest in peace they would have buried me in my La-Z-Boy with a glass of scotch in my hand." This thought makes me smile.

"Let us pray," the minister says. "Compassionate and loving God, we gather to commend Frank Sands into Your most gracious hands. Lift us into the joy and peace of Thy presence. Grief is never an easy burden to bear, but in times like these often it's best to hear from those who were so directly influenced by the departed. So I invite Frank's daughter Jill to share some thoughts of her own."

Jill Sands stands and tugs her jacket down as she walks to the podium. "Hello, everyone, and thank you for being here today," she says, looking up from her notes and nodding at certain individuals in the crowd. "I guess every child knows and fears that this day will come, and yet that doesn't make it any easier or the words any easier to find." She takes a deep breath before looking down again. "Many of you know the wonderful accomplishments of my father. When he came back from Korea, literally starting with one shovel, he built his small construction company into a successful real estate development firm. Over the course of his life he was an active member of the PTA. He was an expert woodworker, an avid wine collector, a gourmet cook, and yet—and yet none of that matters to me today.

"Because all I can think about right now is the time he taught me to drive." She smiles. "One weekend, right before I turned sixteen, he took me out to the parking lot by his office and told me to get behind the wheel. After I'd gotten into the driver's seat and he'd buckled himself in on the passenger side, we sat there for a few minutes not moving and not saying anything. 'You nervous?' he finally asked. And when I nodded my head, he nodded back. 'Good, I thought it was just me,' he laughed. Then he said, 'I could have used a shot of bourbon before I left the house.' 'Me too!' I replied.

"Anyway, when I finally mustered my nerve, I turned the key, put the car in reverse, and stepped on the gas hard. Well, not two seconds later we hear that sickening sound of something being crushed to oblivion beneath the tires. I screamed. Dad screamed. Then he jumped out of the car to see what I'd just killed. And as I sat there for what felt like an eternity—but what was probably three seconds—I silently sent up a prayer that if I hadn't, in fact, killed anything, I'd never drive again. Next thing I know I hear Dad laughing. Turned out I'd only run over a bottle of Coke that had rolled under the car.

"Well, when Dad got back in and told me to start her up again I just shook my head and told him I couldn't. I explained to him the deal I'd just made with God, and that this had probably been God's way of telling me that I shouldn't be on the roads anyway. Dad looked at me very seriously, and then, in that manner that those of us who knew him best would recall, he said, 'Cut the shit, Jilly, and get on with it.'"

Yeah, that does sound like Mr. Sands, I think.

"And that was Dad," Jill continues, laughing herself. Then her breath catches. "That was Frank Sands. A man who was perfect and flawed and wise and selfish. He was smart and he was stubborn and sometimes I hated him. And sometimes he hated me, and a lot of those times he wasn't wrong to do so. But he always taught me the importance of keeping perspective on things. He launched me into the world and taught me to appreciate life. It's how I'll get through today because I know he'd tell me to 'cut the shit' and to keep in mind that he'd led exactly the life he wanted to lead. That he'd married the woman he'd always wanted to be with and they loved each other fiercely. He'd tell me that he had no regrets, that he'd been blessed in life and that it was his time to go. I know how much he valued the members of his extended family and his friendships and I know he thought that's what made life worth living. Thank you all for being here today to honor that memory." Jill gives one of those unhappy smiles, then walks back to her seat.

Isabelle stands and hugs Jill, and the two keep holding on to each other. That's when I feel the tears sliding down my cheeks, and I can't stop them. I cry for the loss of my friend Mr. Sands, who genuinely lived the life he wanted. I cry for my friend Izzy and her loss. I cry for the relationship they had, and for the love they shared through years full of curves. They stayed friends and stayed in love despite it all. I cry because, after all, I think that's what having faith really means.

"In its most raw form today we feel the homily 'the Lord giveth and the Lord taketh away,'" the minister says. "But that we grieve, that we mourn, that's a testament to the impact of that life and it reminds us that though Frank is no longer with us in corporeal form, his spirit remains. Please join me in reciting the twenty-third psalm."

As we start reciting the prayer, I realize how reassuring it is to hear all of those voices coming together, echoing against the marble. Everyone is probably thinking about slightly different things—my mind usually wandered to my own stuff during group prayer—but when everyone chants together, at least your own voice is amplified.

"And let us say, 'Amen.'" *Amen.*

People stand and begin filing out to the main reception area and that's when I catch sight of Jeff Potts from Hanover House.

"Grace," he says, putting his arm around my shoulder and giving it a squeeze. "So good of you to come today."

"Mrs. Sands asked me to," I reply, then add, "But I wanted to come. I couldn't have missed it. Do you come to all of these?"

"No." He shakes his head. "But I probably do go to more funerals than most—occupational hazard," he says in a slightly jokey manner.

"And are they all like this?" I nod my head back toward the room we were just in as the coffin is being wheeled out by some of the maintenance men.

"Uh." Jeff nods, his eyes fixing on a far-off place so that I can tell he's recalling some of the others. "Yes and no. Of course there's a certain similarity just in the prayers that are said—and I think that's done almost as a comfort, you know, like marching orders, so people can sort of mindlessly repeat the message, go through the experience as ritual. But I'll tell you, all you need is one person to really speak from the heart, the way they tell the story of how much a gesture that person did changed their life, influenced their thinking, or touched them in some way, it can just hit you. And phew, it's all over."

Even though this is the first funeral I've been to, I think I know what he means. "Yeah," I say, "I cried when Jill told that story."

"Me too," Jeff replies, then smiles at me.

I wait for him to say something Jeff Potts–like, like, "But don't tell the ladies that," or possibly even more Pottsian, "Now be sure to tell the ladies that so they know I'm a sensitive guy," but he doesn't, and his genuineness makes me like him more. "The Sandses are such good people. They really cared for each other so deeply."

"I just wish they could have found a cure in time to save him."

"I know," he replies. "And I know this may be hard to hear, but considering the suffering and frustration Frank would have faced as the disease progressed, this"—Jeff tilts his head toward the casket—"was almost certainly a godsend."

I press my lips together wondering what Jeff would say if he knew I was involved—me, Grace Manning, "agent of God's will." *A godsend* . . . I doubt it, but it sure would be nice to believe he's right.

◦◦◦

I'm one of the first to arrive back at the Sandses' house, and I volunteer to help prepare some of the fruit platters. I'm concentrating so hard on trying to carve perfectly shaped cantaloupe balls that I jump when I feel a hand on my waist.

"Oh, my," Isabelle says. "I wasn't expecting that."

"Me neither," I reply. "I guess I was sort of in my own little cantaloupe world there for a minute." This makes Isabelle smile, but I feel like I should say something less doofy, considering the circumstances. "It really was a nice service," I say.

"Frank would have approved," she replies. "And he would have been especially gratified by the turnout. Do you know what I did? Counted heads," she says in a low voice. "Isn't that terrible?"

"Would it be terrible to ask how many heads you counted?"

Isabelle smiles, then takes my wet, cantaloupey hand and gives it a squeeze. "Yuck," she says, now looking at her wet hand before wiping it directly on her dress. "See? There are advantages to wearing a frumpy dress after all."

I laugh quietly. "It's really not so bad."

Isabelle rolls her eyes; she's not buying it. "There were about a hundred and eighty people present, give or take. Some of them I could have done without," she says quietly. "Like the old shrews who kept nagging me to get an autopsy to see if there'd been negligence."

"Oh," I say, my breath quickening, "so you didn't do an autopsy?"

"No," she replies. "*We* know what took Frank. His poor body had been through enough and I was going to be damned if I would let anyone disturb him further."

I nod, unable to speak. *We* do know what took Frank, and I feel my shoulders and back unclench. There won't be a probe. There won't be an investigation, a trial, or an official sentence of guilt. Now if only I can find a way to live with *myself.*

"Isabelle, what a beautiful service," a woman says, coming over to us at the sink and putting her arms around her shoulders. "Come, let me make you a sandwich, you must be hungry."

"Really, no, I'm not hungry at all. I think my body knows food wouldn't sit so well right now."

"You have to eat, Iz," she insists. "It'll make you feel better."

"Hardly," she replies, but the woman doesn't take no for an answer, takes Isabelle's hand and leads her into the living room. As she leaves the kitchen, the Sands daughters walk in and I look at them wondering how Lolly and I would be behaving to each other if we were in their position. Do you act like you always have, like nothing's changed? Or do you finally let everything from the past go?

"I'm just going to—" I say to no one in particular,

then pick up my plate of misshapen cantaloupe balls and quickly head out of the kitchen.

"Hey," Cole says, approaching me. He's wearing a navy blue blazer with a gray and blue striped rep tie over gray flannel pants. It's like he stepped out of the J. Crew College Admissions/Funeral Catalog.

"Hi," I say. "Do you want any?" I offer the plate of mangled circle-esque fruit.

"Uh, no, that's okay." He makes a face. "I'm not really hungry. You want to go outside or something?" He loosens his tie and unbuttons his top button as we walk out the door. The catalog model look is now complete. We sit down on the porch stairs and look out over the rest of the Hanover House complex.

"I got to spend a lot of time with your grandfather," I say. "He was a really great guy. And your grandmother, she's amazing too."

"I never really spent a lot of time with them myself," Cole replies. "But do you know they were married almost twice as long as they were single?"

"It's kind of amazing. All my relationships seem to break up after the first kiss."

"Well, I guess we know what that means," says Cole, nodding his head.

"No, what?"

"You must be an awful kisser." When he laughs, I freeze. It's as if Cole's channeling Mr. Sands. The delivery, the sound of his laugh, it sounds just like his grandfather. "Uh, I was just kidding," Cole adds when he sees the expression on my face. "I mean, I'm sure you're great at it." He grins impishly, and Mr. Sands flashes through again.

I need to say something clever; I need to hear that laugh again.

"Yeah, you know what they say, 'Kissing is just the best way of getting people so close they can't see what's wrong with each other.'" Cole nods and smiles at this, but it makes me think about Eric and all that's gone on between us. I think about how long we've been friends, and yet how quickly things seemed to have changed between us. *How is it possible that something that took years to build could break so fast?* Then I think about my mom and dad, and wonder how long their relationship was breaking before it gave out. And that makes me think about Mr. and Mrs. Sands, and how long their relationship lasted before I came along and shattered it to pieces. "I should get back inside to see if they need any help," I say. But when I try to stand up, I feel my heart throbbing. I put my hand up to my chest and try to catch my breath.

"Hey, are you okay?"

That's the last thing I hear.

Chapter Seventeen

One of the super-vivid memories I have of my dad is when I fell off a jungle gym after Little League practice years ago. Practice had just ended, and a bunch of us ran to the field's nearby monkey bars as we waited for some parents to arrive and for those who were already there to stop their jabbering and drive us home. I'd been hanging upside down, showing off for no one in particular, when I took that spectacular spill, hitting a hard patch of mud, splitting my lip and scraping most of the skin off my knee and chin. Dad hadn't been that far away, but his back was turned, and as I came crashing to the earth I can remember the sound of his laughter mixing with that of another mother's on the playground. It took a second for my brain to register what had happened, but as soon as it did, and the pain rocketed through my body, I started to wail. When my tears mixed with snot and the taste of blood and caused me to shriek even louder, Dad came running toward me, his dark hair flopping around his face as he ran. When Dad reached me he scooped me into his arms and started rocking me back and forth, trying to make me stop crying. It was as if he thought I was still an infant and this would be the magic cure. It worked. By his simply being there, I knew I'd be okay.

That's the taste I have in my mouth when I open my eyes and feel Isabelle's cool hand on my forehead. The room is dark, but I can see we're alone in her bedroom.

"You gave us quite a scare there," Isabelle says, smiling down at me.

I reach my fingers to my lip, which feels puffy under a small bandage. "What happened?"

"You made Cole move more quickly than I ever knew he was capable," she laughs. "He said you two had just been chatting out on the porch, and when you tried to stand you fainted. You hit your chin on the step when you came down. Gave it a good wallop. How does it feel?"

"My whole head hurts."

"I think you came down pretty hard. The old ladies around here wanted to take you over to the hospital facility on the grounds, get you looked at by some of the doctors. But I knew you'd live, so I didn't want to take any chances by sending you over there." She smiles, pointing her head in the direction of the main house.

I look at Isabelle and realize I have to tell her the truth; whatever happens to me when she hears it, happens. I can't live with this secret any longer. It's time for me to take responsibility for my actions.

"Isabelle, there's something I need to tell you, but I'm

not sure . . . I mean, I don't know how to tell you except just to say it."

"Well, whatever it is, Grace, there's no need to be embarrassed. You know there are no judgments here," she says, patting my hand.

I swallow, but my throat is completely dry. "I . . ." I shut my eyes, not wanting to see the look on her face when I finally say it: "I killed him."

"What?"

I open my eyes and see Isabelle has recoiled, her back straightening like a rod. "I'm sorry. I . . . He asked me to help him."

"Oh, Grace, oh my god, no," Isabelle replies, the back of her hand covering her mouth. She stands and turns away from me, walking toward the window.

"I'm so sorry. I thought—"

"No, Grace, no."

I am desperate to explain, desperate to not lose Isabelle too. "It wasn't my idea. I mean originally I told him no. I didn't want to do it." I can feel a lump rise in my throat and lodge there. "But he kept getting worse, and I knew that was exactly what scared him the most. I just thought it would be merciful. Isabelle, I'm so sorry. I thought helping him die was the right thing to do."

"Don't say that," she says again, this time much more quietly. Isabelle walks over to the door and pulls it closed, then turns back to me and comes over to the bed. She sits down and doesn't say anything for what feels like an eternity. Then she bows her head. "You *weren't* responsible for Frank's death, Grace. You just weren't."

"No, I'm telling you." I wonder how much detail I should give her. "He gave me some pills—"

"Grace, you didn't kill him," she says sternly.

I stare at Isabelle. I think she must be so distraught, she doesn't even realize what she's saying. "Look, Izzy, I mean thank you for saying that, but I made the decision to help him take the pills. You have to know that."

"Grace, I knew. I knew that's what Frank wanted."

"What? You knew? This whole time?"

"No, no. I meant I knew he *wanted* to ask you to help him, but *not* that he actually asked. Oh, Grace, I can't tell you how horrible I feel about this," Isabelle says, balling her hand to her mouth as her body starts rocking back and forth.

"I'm . . . confused."

Isabelle pauses for a moment to regain her composure, but still won't meet my eyes. "The day after you and I first met, I asked Frank more about you and he just went on and on about what a great young lady you were." Isabelle stops, then finally looks back up at me. "Now, don't get me wrong, since I've gotten to know you, I completely understand why Frank was so enthusiastic. But on that day I found it quite odd that my husband was making such a fuss," she says. "So I pressed him on it. I said, 'Tell me what it is you like so much about Grace.' And Frank wouldn't elaborate. He tried joking around. Told me I was jealous of a pretty young girl! Maybe I even was a little."

"You were jealous of *me*? Why?"

A smile fixes on Isabelle's face. "Grace, I'd been married to that man for almost fifty years and yet in the last years, since his health had been declining, there was nothing I could do to make him feel any better. It wasn't for lack of trying, believe me! But he was just getting sicker and we both saw the life was washing out of him. That someone else had managed to make him happy during this time, well, that upset me a bit, I confess. Though this is all somewhat beside the point now." She shakes her head and rubs her hands against her legs before continuing. "Anyway, as I was saying, I pressed him on it, brought up your name again. That's when he said you were a person of great character, he trusted you . . . I just had a terrible feeling that I knew what that meant to him." Isabelle stops for a moment.

"What do you mean by that?" I ask, still feeling guilty and defensive.

"Grace, Frank and I had always promised each other that if things ever became too painful, too awful to go on, we would . . . well, help each other. We'd made that pledge when we were in our prime and healthy, though. I just never really thought—I never really thought that I'd be in the position where it'd become a necessity. You learn not to dwell on these things. You can't. You have to live for the day, so you just put them out of your head as best you can."

I shrug my shoulders. "I guess."

"Well, a few months back, when it had become clear that he wasn't getting any better—nor would he—he reminded me of our pact." Isabelle fidgets in her seat and starts wringing her hands. I'd never thought that term "wringing her hands" could be so literal before, but Isabelle actually looks like she's trying to squeeze something out of them, like water or blood.

"He said to me, 'Izzy, you and I, we had a deal,'" she continues. "But I wouldn't have it. I pretended like I didn't hear it, and acted like I didn't know what he was referring to, which, of course was a damn lie. And that's when he said that if I wouldn't help him, he'd find someone who would. I never thought he'd go through with it, Grace, and please, please believe me that I had no idea he seriously considered approaching you—" Isabelle reaches for my hand. "I mean, to think he'd ask a child to do something like . . ." She trails off again and shakes her head, sobbing quietly.

I don't know if I'm supposed to just let her continue, tell her something to make her feel better, or just start screaming. But my throat feels paralyzed, I'm so thrown by what I'm hearing.

She takes a tissue out of her sleeve and wipes the corners of her eyes. "I can't tell you how angry this makes me, Grace," Isabelle says, her eyes piercing mine.

"I didn't mean to make you mad," I reply lamely.

"No, dear, I'm not mad at you. I'm mortified, horrified by him. By my husband. That he would put something like that on you. It's not like he was asking you to fetch his slippers or air out the room." Isabelle stands and starts pacing around. "Once or twice, I admit, I had twinges that he might have actually said something to you, but I just couldn't bring myself to think that of a man I'd loved. That he'd put such a burden on your shoulders, it's monstrous."

"Well, why didn't you just ask me?"

"I don't know, part of me thought this was a private thing between my husband and me, and asking you meant a break in my trust of him. Now, of course, I see I should have asked. That would have been the right thing to do, but"—she looks to me with a twisted smile—"I suppose it was also easier for me to pretend as long as I blocked out the possibility, it couldn't happen."

"I know how you feel," I reply. "The whole time I kept wondering if you knew or if you were totally in the dark. And I didn't know how you felt about the whole thing in the first place."

She comes back down to the bed and crosses her legs, then begins picking at the hem of her dress. "The last thing I wanted was for you to have to struggle with this. Grace, he was a very ill man. Everyone kept saying he was on 'borrowed time.' Borrowed time, I hate that phrase." She shakes her head. "But the truth was, he was in hell there at the end. That he died wasn't your fault."

The more Isabelle tries to excuse it—the more she condones my decision to help—the more it's making me feel like I need to tell her all the details of how it went down. Even if she knew, I was still responsible. "I went into his room that night," I say, looking away from her. "And I took the pills he gave me and smashed them up and—"

"No, Grace, you don't understand what I mean. I mean pills or no pills, you aren't the one responsible for his death. I am." Isabelle puts her hand under my chin so that I have to look at her. "I am."

"But I gave him the pills," I say.

"I disconnected his respirator," she replies, tears starting to leak from the corners of her eyes.

"What?"

"The evening he passed, that's when *I* finally made the decision to help him. I felt enough was enough. I knew the man I'd loved my whole life would be incredibly angry at me if I let him languish like that. I couldn't stand that idea. So I made the decision. I'd watched the nurses enough times to know how to disable the alarm on the respirator. Those machines beeped so frequently when nothing was wrong, they'd come into the room, push a few buttons on the front panel, and stop the noise. So that's what I did after I loosened the con-

nection on his respirator. Then I said my final good-bye
to Frank and left the room. I should have stayed, but
I couldn't be there to watch the life go out of my love."
Isabelle stops talking and closes her eyes. "You must
have come in after I left."

"How long does it take for a person to die after the
respirator is disconnected?" I ask, trying to do the time
line in my head: When did Isabelle pull ("*loosen*") the
plug compared to when I gave him the pill mixture?
Who *really* killed him?

"Well, I'm no expert, but my understanding is that it
varies from person to person. I think it depends on how
greatly they were relying on the machine to breathe for
them," she replies. "Apparently some people pass a few
minutes after the artificial ventilation stops. With others, it can take a few hours up to several days or even
weeks." Isabelle looks at me and can no doubt see this
wasn't quite the answer I was hoping for. "But, Grace,"
she continues, "I must tell you, each step of the way I
talked Frank through it. I explained what I was doing
because I felt that once he knew I'd done my part, he'd
marshal his will and take care of the rest as quickly
as he could. Knowing my husband, I feel sure that he
would have wanted all of our suffering to end as quickly
as possible. When I came back to his room very early
the next morning it was over."

"Have you told anyone else about this?"

"No," she replies. "This was one of the last things my

husband and I needed to do together. I didn't want anyone else's input or thoughts on the subject. It wasn't any of their business. Oh, Grace, can you ever forgive me?"

"Yes, of course I forgive you. How could I not?"

"Thank you," she says.

She then takes my hand and we sit there for a while, both of us lost in our own thoughts, together. As she looks down, I look up and think about the new chance I've been given, and how much I have to be grateful for.

"Thank you," I whisper to the universe.

Chapter Eighteen

Later that night I stare in my bedroom mirror examining the bruise on my chin. I'd not only clipped my chin when I'd fainted, I also bit down on my lip, making it look slightly swollen, and not in a good way. As I try to determine if putting lipstick over it will make it look better or worse, the phone rings.

"Hey, it's me," Eric says when I pick up.

"Oh, hi." Oh, man.

"We need to talk."

I know what he's referring to, of course. I think about what Isabelle had said about how dumb it is to try to avoid conversations like this. But sometimes even knowing what the right thing is doesn't make doing it any easier. "I thought we already talked about that," I say. "Natalie came over, 'attacked' you, and now you guys are like 'couple of the year.'"

Eric exhales loudly. "Look, I know you're pissed."

"I'm not pissed," I lie, flopping down on my bed.

"Okay, maybe that's the wrong word then."

I bite down on my lip and a twinge of pain from the bruise radiates through my jaw. "Actually, 'pissed' is fair."

"You know I debated whether I should tell you about it at all. Ninety-eight percent of me said, 'Don't do it, nothing good will come of it.' But the other two percent somehow managed to convince me that I should." He lets out one of those little laughs that makes it sound like he's marveling over his own stupidity. "I wish I could tell you that that two percent was the good angel sitting on my shoulder, saying, 'Tell her the truth, honesty is the best policy!' but I don't think that was it. I think part of me really just wanted to get a rise out of you. Make you mad."

"Nice job."

"Grace, things have been totally bizarre between the two of us recently."

"I know, and it's been my fault, I get it. This whole thing with Natalie is like my punishment for being weird or something, right?"

"No, that's not it. I didn't want to punish you. Maybe I just wanted to get a real reaction from you."

"That's great, Eric, thanks."

"Grace, come on."

"What do you want me to say? That I'm happy for you? I'm sorry, Eric, I know maybe as your friend I'm supposed to be psyched for you that you're hooking up with the hottest girl at school. I mean, I know that's some big accomplishment. And I know how other girls look at you now, like Chelsea Roy and all the rest. It's like they've suddenly 'discovered' you and now see what a great, cool guy you are. But it didn't take me seeing you toss a ball through a hoop to realize that. I always knew it and I just thought, I don't know, maybe that we had something. Or—"

"Or what?"

"Or it doesn't even matter now, so let's just drop it."

"I'm not going to drop it. Look, Natalie just called me because she wanted to talk about us going to the dance together."

"Oh yeah? So have you two color coordinated your outfits yet?"

"I told her I wasn't going to go after all."

"Perfect," I laugh bitterly. "Now I can have her all to myself! But I'll bet people will be dying to know how someone like me managed to get a date with a girl as hot as her."

"Grace, stop," Eric says. "I never wanted to go to that dance with Natalie. You know that. I asked you, remember?"

"But that was before you knew you could have her." I stand again and look at myself in the mirror. All I can see is damage.

"I don't want her! I don't want Chelsea or anybody else," Eric yells. "Don't you get it? It's you. I want you."

♪ ♪ ♪

And that's when I tell Eric everything. That's when I tell him what had been going on with Mr. Sands. That's when I tell him about my last conversation with Isabelle.

"Holy shit," replies Eric.

"Yeah, I've said that a few times myself."

"So you're not the one who *actually* killed him, are you?" he asks.

"That's kind of a tough question to answer."

Eric pauses, and I listen for the judgment in the sound of his breathing. But when he speaks again he simply says, "I'm just trying to imagine what I would have done if I were you . . . I don't know."

"Well," I reply, "you probably would have thought about it for a long time and then you would have come to some conclusion that factored in quality of life and personal responsibility and morality and divine intervention and family and love and suffering and autonomy and fairness and consequences. And after weighing all that, you still might not have known what the right answer was, or if there *is* a right answer at all. But hopefully whatever you chose to do you'd feel like it was a good decision. So if I haven't quite been myself lately, that's probably why. I've had a few things on my mind."

"Yeah, just a few," he says, with a disbelieving laugh. "There anything else you've been thinking about that I should know?"

"Uh, just one more thing."

"*Seriously?*" Eric doesn't sound like he can stand

to hear any more, but I need to tell him this one last thing.

"I never got a chance to say how much you being there for me every day has meant to me."

"You don't have to."

"I know," I say, "which is part of why I want to."

♪ ♪ ♪

On Friday night I reach deep into my closet and feel around for the Cignal bag that I'd thrown to the back as soon as I'd gotten home from my shopping trip the other day. I hadn't allowed myself to touch it again and tried not to think about the red silk dress wrapped inside. It was a present to myself that after purchase I felt sure I didn't deserve, and though I'm still not sure I deserve it, I am sure wearing the dress will make me "better." Or at least look better. In keeping with that theme, for the past several days I've been trying to eat better too. Or at least eat less. I cleaned out all my pockets of junk food and tossed the candy I'd stashed around the house.

When I finally free the Cignal bag from the mountain of crap at the bottom of the closet, I carefully remove its tissue-papered contents. I slide my finger under the sticker seal and pull the protective sheets back. My breath catches when I see the beautiful red silk fabric shining up at me. If possible, the dress is prettier than I remembered. I hold it against me and glance at myself in the mirror, wanting to preserve the image of what I could look like before trying the dress on in case the Cinderella moment doesn't happen, and the dress doesn't fit so perfectly again.

But after I slip off my robe and step into it, I know its magic is working because the zipper closes easily—in one fluid movement—even without me taking a deep inhale. I spin on my heels and I watch in the full-length mirror as the dress twirls around me. It takes less than a second to spot a critical error: shoes. Now if I happened to own shoes other than Pumas or Chuck Taylors, this would not be such a big deal. The problem is that the only shoes I own are rubber soled and ink tattooed, and even the thought of putting them anywhere near this beautiful dress is just wrong. I'm shoeless, and it's an hour and a half before the dance.

What's almost worse is that I can picture the perfect pair for the dress: black sequined T-straps, piped with vintage-looking silver leather with a high red satin stiletto heel. These shoes are an outfit to themselves. And they're sitting at the top of Mom's closet in a box that hasn't been reopened since Mom and Dad's twentieth anniversary party last year.

For the many differences between the Manning women, we all have size 7½ feet, so I know they'd fit me. I consider my options: I could sneak into Mom's bedroom, take the shoes, and pray they don't get scuffed or spilled on, returning them to the box when she's out tomorrow. I could take the box and stick it in Lolly's closet, assuming that by the time Mom ever goes looking for them (presumably no time soon), the two of them would work it out. Or I could go downstairs, ask her to borrow them, and do the right thing.

This is not a decision I make quickly. But in light of all the rest, I decide to try harder on this front too.

"Mom?" I call as I walk down the steps, assuming she's in the kitchen.

"My stars," she says, glancing up from her magazine. Mom's camped out on the couch in a pair of sweats and fuzzy slippers. "Look at you."

"Oh." I'm immediately self-conscious and worried she's about to ask where I got the dress or how I managed to pay for it on my own. I'd never bothered bringing up the subject of it or the dance again after we'd fought about it. "Does it look okay?"

"Does it look *okay*? It's gorgeous." Mom motions me to the couch, then shuts her magazine and sits up. "Oh, Grace, I don't think you've ever looked prettier."

"Thanks," I say, pleased and a little surprised.

Mom laughs. "So I guess this means you and Eric worked things out, huh? Or are you going with someone else and this dress is designed to make him regret that decision?"

"No, Eric and I talked and kind of figured some things out."

"I'm glad to hear that. It's good to know you were both smart enough to make up. I'm proud of you."

"You are?"

"Of course I am," she replies. "Especially because I know I haven't been the best role model for this sort of stuff. I mean, I wish I were better at it, and I have to think if your dad and I could have given you a happier example, this would just be easier all around, but . . ." Mom shrugs, unable to finish the sentence. "Just to be clear, though, you do know that I'm on your side and that I love you, right?"

"Yeah," I say, "most of the time."

Mom tips her head side to side as if considering this. "That's fair." She doesn't ask if I mean that I think she's on my side most of the time, or whether she means some of the time she's not. But I think we both get it.

Still, I'm a little scared that asking to borrow Mom's special anniversary party shoes will immediately march us two steps back, so I send up a silent prayer that she won't hit the roof when I mention them. "Hey, uh, Mom?"

"Yeah?"

"So there's one little problem." I point to my bare feet. Before I can even mention borrowing her shoes, a smile comes across her face.

"I have the *perfect* solution!" she says, hopping off the couch, taking my hand, and leading me upstairs. Mom flips the light on in her bedroom and I realize I haven't been in here much over the past few months. Though we've all been living under the same roof, we've pretty much existed in our own pods.

Minus the T-shirts Dad usually left in piles at the corners of the room, and the various objects he'd clear out of his pockets and spread on his dresser, the room hasn't changed much. As Mom walks over to her closet, I glance at her bureau and see she still hasn't moved the silver framed wedding photo of her and Dad that's been there forever. In the photo Mom and Dad are looking at each other as they're exiting the church just after they were married. Dad is dressed in one of those old-fashioned tuxedos and he's gazing at Mom like she's the only woman on earth. Mom beams back at him, looking like it would be impossible for her to be any happier. I assumed that the photo would have been the first thing to go after Dad left. But seeing it sitting there on dresser, making it look like nothing has changed when, in fact, *everything* has changed, causes a new lump to form in the back of my throat.

Mom turns around and catches me staring at the photo. She walks over and lets out a long breath. "I know," she says, "I keep thinking I should put it away. But every time I pick it up to shove it in a drawer, I wind up putting it right back there."

"Well, it's a great picture," I reply, thinking about what Isabelle said about missing Mr. Sands, and how hard it must be to let go.

"Look at us. So full of hope for our lives together." She shakes her head and smiles. "I think part of the reason I haven't packed the picture away is because I like seeing that hope in my eyes. I know your father's gone, and it's not just about pining for him anymore. It's also about me, and reminding myself that happiness like this is possible."

"I get that. And I'm a believer too."

"Thank you, honey," Mom says, reaching out and squeezing my arm. "Now, on to another very important matter." From behind her back Mom reveals a pristine gray shoebox. "Ta-da!" She holds on to the bottom of the box as I remove the lid, and yin-yanged inside is the perfect pair of shoes. I take each shoe from the box and slide into them before bending over and buckling their T-straps. They're so high, I almost fall forward as I stand back up, but Mom catches my arm and prevents me from face-planting in her carpet.

"Mom, they're amazing."

"And only worn once. Not exactly my everyday fare," she laughs. "Okay, stand back so I can get a good look at you."

I take a few steps backward and stretch my arms out like a model presenting a prize. "What do you think?"

"I think you have one very lucky date." She smiles.

"Thanks," I say, feeling a big, goofy grin come across my face.

Mom looks at her watch. "Hey, have you eaten dinner yet?"

"Well, I was thinking maybe I should skip it so the dress doesn't bulge out or anything."

"Come on," she says with a shake of her head. "You need to eat something before you go. You know, I saw the griddle in the dish rack. What do you say to me fixing us a quick pancake dinner?"

I run my hands down my hips and consider this for a moment. "I probably shouldn't."

"How about this," she persists, "I'll make a stack and you just have one?"

"Eat only one pancake! Is that even possible?"

"It'll be a challenge," Mom says with a nod, taking my hand and leading me downstairs. "But, you know what? I have faith in you."

♪ ♪ ♪

When the doorbell rings I actually feel my heart beating in my chest. I stand up from the kitchen table and look at Mom.

"Do you want me to get the door?" she asks, smiling.

"No, I got it, thanks." I smile back at her and keep my eyes on my feet as I walk to the front door. "Who is it?" I say, trying to catch my breath as I look through the peephole and see Eric standing there, holding a bouquet of flowers.

"Pizza delivery."

I laugh as I swing open the door and Eric stands there smiling back at me.

"Wow," he says. "You look . . . wow."

"Thanks," I reply, blush starting to rise in my cheeks, which probably matches the redness of my dress. As soon as I'd slipped it on earlier, and the silk fabric rubbed against my bare skin, I got all goose-bumpy, which is pretty much how I'm feeling right now.

"Ooh, let me get a picture!" Mom says as she walks out of the kitchen.

"*Mom!*" I howl on reflex.

"Come on," Eric says, nudging me with his shoulder, "I bet it'll only hurt a little."

When I look at him, and we give each other our conspiratorial sideways smiles, she snaps the picture.

♪ ♪ ♪

The tables in the cafeteria have all been folded and neatly stacked in the back corner behind the DJ stand. The lights are down and even though the space is still very perceptibly the place where crimes against humanity are served for lunch every day, even the grouch in me must admit that the decorating committee has done a really nice job. Against the back wall they've hung a black mural that's been painted to resemble the night sky. Small white stars glitter when the light from the suspended, rotating mirror ball shines against them. I'd forgotten the theme was supposed to be "dancing under the stars," but they've somehow managed to pull it off, lending the cafeteria a surprisingly dreamy feel.

I immediately see Lolly and Jake on the dance floor, her arms around his neck and his holding tightly around her waist. They're swaying to the music, a song that's not really slow enough to slow dance to, but neither of them seems to care. Looking at them you'd never know that there'd been any recent relationship problems, you'd never realize that Jake had originally wanted to be here with someone else. Of course, I wish Lolly had been strong enough to realize she didn't need Jake and that she would have been better off without him. But there's a giant smile on her face, and it's obvious how happy she is now.

I can't help but feel he's going to hurt her again. I'm sure of it even as I watch her put her head on his shoulder and he tilts his head so it's sort of nestled into hers. If it were up to me I'd banish him to another school, or better yet another state. But I know it's not up to me, and I know that this is one of those things that despite the best arguments I present to my sister, she's not going to pay me any attention. This is one of those serenity things that I'm just going to have to accept. It's strange—I used to think that as I got older people would just necessarily take what I had to say more seriously. Or my opinions would be listened to. But mostly people just do what they want—follow some sort of interior voice, whatever that happens to be for them, and I guess part of the process of growing up (if that's what it is) is learning to accept that people often want different things.

When the song changes to something more up-tempo, I take off my coat and turn to Eric. "Do you want to dance?"

"Uh, I'm not sure I'm ready to dance quite yet," he replies. "I think I need to warm up a bit first. You know, do some stretching."

"Totally. I wouldn't want you to pull a hamstring."

"I promise we won't flower against the wall all night," he says. "But trust me, you don't want me anywhere near you during a fast song. Not only would you risk physical injury, but I could potentially scar you psychologically, as well."

"Well, look who it is," Jake says as he and Lolly walk off the dance floor. Lolly and I hadn't seen each other before the dance because one of Jake's friends was having a pre-party, so she was out before I'd even gotten home that afternoon.

"Hi, Jake. Hi, Lolly," I reply.

"When did you get here?" she asks, looking me up and down. "And did Mom buy you that dress?"

"We got here about a minute ago," Eric replies for us. "Matter of fact, I've barely had time to show her off and make the other guys here jealous of my great-looking date."

"He's right." Lolly smiles. "You look beautiful. You too, Eric. You clean up pretty good."

"Thanks. Right back atcha." Eric smiles.

The song changes again and Jake squeezes Lolly's hand. "Lol, come on, I love this song," he says.

"Okay." She shrugs her shoulders and turns to the dance floor. Jake walks ahead, but Lolly turns back to Eric and me. "So I'll just let you two stand here awkwardly together now, each of you admiring how hot the other looks, both of you too scared to act on it." And with that, she flits off to find Jake and shimmies seamlessly into the crowd.

Although Eric and I had been perfectly comfortable and jokey with each other a minute ago, now, as Lolly predicted, we're silent.

"Don't laugh at me for saying this, okay?" Eric says. "But I'm really glad we came tonight."

"Because it's a good idea to see and be seen by your teammates?" I ask. Eric shakes his head and smiles. I smile back, knowing that there's no place more I'd rather be than standing next to him right now. "I'm glad we came too."

"It just feels right being here with you," he says. "Do you want to sit down?" Eric asks, and when I nod, he takes my hand and leads me over to the chairs farthest from the speakers. His palm is a little moist, but it doesn't matter, because right now it just feels good against my skin; feels like there's warmth and life pulsing through it.

When we get over to the chairs, we sit down, but Eric

doesn't let my hand go, and I think just how all right it would be if we sat here the rest of the night, hand in hand.

"Is this weird?" he finally says, looking at me.

"A little," I say, "but weird good."

"Fantastic," he replies with a smile, "just the mood I was hoping to set."

"You know what I mean," I say, giving him a little tap on the chest. I let my hand rest there for a moment and he puts his other hand on top of it, holding it against him.

A couple of songs play as we sit there not talking, just being together. And I realize how lucky I am. I also realize how quickly things can change, both for the good and, well, otherwise. It's scary to think about things like that, especially now as I'm feeling happier than I have in as long as I can remember. But I now also know that it's as important to keep this in mind, particularly during the days when things seem darkest. Because living through each moment brings you closer to new light. It might not make things better right then, but having faith that it will helps.

"Come on," Eric says when that old Cure song "Just Like Heaven" starts playing. He stands and starts walking to the dance floor as others stream off.

I put my arms around his neck, and he rests his around my hips, smiling at me as he does this.

"Weird but good." He nods.

"Come here," I reply, smiling widely before I reach up and kiss him.

This, actually, doesn't feel weird at all. It just feels good. I think that's what Isabelle would tell me it's supposed to feel like, and that makes me smile.

"What?" Eric asks, feeling my lips curl up. "Am I doing something wrong?"

"Un-uh." Out of the corner of my eye I see Natalie, who is now standing alone watching us. "Hey, did you want to dance with her?" I say, tilting my head in Natalie's direction.

"No," he replies. "No, Grace, I told you, and I will continue to tell you I want to be here with you."

"Good," I say.

"Good." He nods again.

And it is.

ACKNOWLEDGMENTS

A FEW EARLY READERS DESERVE HEARTFELT THANKS: Kate Morgenroth and Alison Pace were extraordinary note-givers and generous with their time. They not only gave sharp advice, they gave me hope the book would float. Renée Kaplan, among other things, helped me realize that my first title was a loser, and that I really needed to find something catchier. To her I not only owe thanks, but a lifetime supply of pancakes.

Whether it was luck or divine intervention that brought me to Talia Rosenblatt Cohen, my brilliant agent, that's still TBD. But I was incredibly fortunate to work with her and when she left the biz, the angels wept (and I did a little too). Tamar Rydzinski stepped into Talia's big shoes, and she also deserves thanks.

My talented editor, Kate Harrison, invested blood, sweat, and years in this book. Kate agonized over every single word of this bad boy with me. Her dedication was astonishing and she brought the book to a different level. A big bow to her.

Thank you, Amy Epstein Feldman, my super-cool sister, who makes every day more fun. Thanks to Len, Maddie, Benjy, and Eli Feldman for all the love. To Jay Dyckman because he's my favorite heartthrob and always makes me laugh. And my parents, Marcia and Paul Epstein, get my deepest gratitude for, well, for everything. They've been role models and sounding boards, and their love and support continue to "warm the cockles of my heart."